Ashley's Allegiance

Book 5 in the Emerald Springs Legacy

ROBYN NEELEY, author of
Destination Wedding and *Christmas Dinner*

CRIMSON
ROMANCE

F+W Media, Inc.

Published by
Crimson Romance
an imprint of F+W Media, Inc.
10151 Carver Road, Suite 200
Blue Ash, OH 45242. U.S.A.
www.crimsonromance.com

ISBN 10: 1-4405-7105-8
ISBN 13: 978-1-4405-7105-3
eISBN 10: 1-4405-7106-6
eISBN 13: 978-1-4405-7106-0

Acknowledgments

A huge thank you to the Emerald Springs Legacy authors who built a fabulous world that *I*, as the final author, had so much fun playing in: Monica Tillery (*Adam's Ambition*); Holley Trent (*Colleen's Choice*); Elley Arden (*Chad's Chance*); and Nicole Flockton (*Daniel's Decision*).

From Cherry Berry Spice tea and sassy rain boots to Porch Swing beer and Pavlova (Google it!), I had a blast incorporating their characters, their stories, and special nuances into this final book.

A very special thank you to Crimson Romance editor, Julie Sturgeon, for making all of these stories shine.

CHAPTER ONE

Deputy Sheriff Jacob Sanders didn't know what he did to deserve this, but it could arguably be the best day of his life.

"Uncuff me." Ashley Whitman twisted her hands from behind her back. "This is so not happening." She stood outside the Emerald Springs sheriff's station in a skin revealing, pink tank top and tight black yoga pants. Her long, wavy blonde hair curved around her neck in a messy ponytail. "You can't arrest me."

Jacob stood behind her, trying his best to hide the smile that threatened any minute to overtake his entire face. He'd waited for a moment like this since high school. Now that it was here, he wanted to savor every single, glorious second.

Ashley blew out a breath. "Are you going to stand back there? Say something."

"Okay, princess." His voice was deep and in control. "This is how it's going to work. I'll escort you inside where we'll be taking your picture. Then one of those French nails of yours will get a little dirty."

"You're fingerprinting me?" She struggled. "This is ridiculous. You can't arrest me. I'm … I'm … I'm a Whitman!"

Jacob threw his head back and let out a hearty laugh. Watching Ashley squirm was priceless. "Don't think your pedigree is going to help you out now." It was typical of her to insinuate that her Whitman status somehow made her superior. He'd grown up with that.

"Whatever. When do I get my phone call?"

"After I hand you over." Truth be told, he'd already gone ahead and made *that* call for her while she stewed in the backseat of his squad car. That person should be arriving any second.

As if on cue, Chad Whitman zipped into the parking lot in his Jeep Wrangler. The sides and top had been chucked and an indie rock tune blared from the radio. While Jacob enjoyed riding shotgun along with his buddy every once in a while through the dirt roads of the Skagit Valley, he had busted Chad a time or two for his alternative taste. He was more a country music, boots kickin' kind of guy.

The youngest of the Whitman boys and his pal since high school, Chad would be the best one to come and get Ashley after Jacob was done messing with her. God knows she probably wouldn't allow him to drive her home. He'd hinted to Chad it wasn't anything serious and that he was just teaching her a lesson.

Chad jumped out of his Jeep and greeted them. "I knew this day would come. What'd my beautiful cousin do, deputy?" he deadpanned.

"Nothing," Ashley responded through gritted teeth. "I did absolutely nothing to deserve this law enforcement brutality."

Chad looked down at her cuffed hands. "Geez, Ashley, it's only 9:00 a.m."

"Just get me out of these." She nodded behind her shoulder.

"Care to fill me in?" Chad asked Jacob. Ashley couldn't see the smirk on his face.

"It was all a misunderstanding," she answered for him.

Jacob laughed sarcastically. "I wouldn't exactly call assaulting an officer of the law a misunderstanding."

"Oh, please. I barely touched you." She turned to Chad. "Some of the girls, including your bride-to-be, were doing stretches in the park. We do a little Zumba a few mornings before work. That's hardly a crime. I'm certified, for God's sake."

Chad raised a curious eyebrow. "That's where Jen ran off to at the crack of dawn?"

Jacob had forgotten that his buddy was newly engaged. Lucky man. Jen had turned his own head when she first blew into town. He'd never admit that to Chad.

Ashley glared at Jacob. "Some of the girls asked me to help them get in shape for Zoe and Adam's wedding."

"Jen doesn't need it," Chad retorted. "She's perfect just the way she is."

Jacob jumped in. "Um … can we get back to the issue at hand?" He adjusted his deputy hat. It'd been raining in Emerald Springs over the last week, but today the morning sun beat down on his head. "We've had some complaints."

"Complaints?" Chad asked.

Ashley sighed. "So our music was a bit loud. I'll turn it down next time."

Jacob smirked. "I'm not talking about the music." His gaze slid up Ashley's workout attire, resting on her pink top. Actually, more like workout bra. Wrapped around her chest, it didn't leave much to the imagination. Not that Jacob thought of her in that way. It was *Ashley Whitman,* after all. On a good day she got under his skin.

Chad grew impatient. "Then what did they do? Is Jen in trouble? I should call her." He reached in his pocket for his cell phone.

Ashley wiggled her hands behind her back. "Um … earth to Chad. She's not the one in handcuffs. Your innocent cousin could use a little help here!"

Jacob tried his best not to smile at the Christmas present in front of him. Not ready to return it, he grabbed Ashley's arm and led her inside the station. "There have been some complaints about the women showing off too much skin," he explained, pointing to Ashley's top. "They've been distracting the men's running club."

"Seriously?" Chad raised a more than curious eyebrow. "The men have been complaining?"

Jacob laughed. "More like their wives."

Ashley rolled her eyes. "Oh, please. It's not like we're sleeping with any of their husbands."

Chad came up beside her and yanked her pony tail. "None of you better be. So why did you hit Jacob?"

Ashley shrugged.

"She wouldn't leave, so I grabbed her arm. That's when she went all Fight Club." Jacob karate-chopped the air.

"I barely touched you. Trust me, Jacob Sanders, there would be a mark if I hit you hard."

Chad inserted himself between the two, pulling Jacob aside to talk privately. "Okay, you and I know that you are not going to arrest her. Can you take the handcuffs off before she totally loses it?"

Jacob smirked at his buddy. Although the feud between the Sanderses and the Whitmans ran deep since their fathers dissolved their partnership in WhitSand Farm twenty years ago, Jacob had never held a grudge. His sister, Colleen, on the other hand, would rather starve than eat anything containing ingredients from the Whitman farm. Now that she seemed to be craving everything in sight, perhaps her taste buds would cave in.

He'd grown up hanging out with Chad and his two older brothers, Adam and Daniel, and he and Chad had played varsity baseball together in high school. Still friends, they would often catch a game at The Rusty Tap over beers.

"Hey, how's engagement life?" he asked, prolonging the inevitable release of the blonde spitfire.

Chad grinned. "It's freakin' awesome. You should try it sometime."

"Nah." Jacob shook his head. That wouldn't be happening anytime soon. "I think I'm more suited for the bachelor life. No one to bail out of trouble." His gaze rested on Ashley. "No one to get on your nerves …"

"So, you going to let her go soon?" Chad asked. "I need to drop her off at her condo and then get to the diner. Jen and I have a meeting with the staff to go over the summer menu and update them on the microbrewery."

"How's that going?" Jacob asked. As the manager of Emerald Eats, Chad had recently begun renovations to expand the family diner to include a microbrewery. Jen would soon run the restaurant as the brewmistress with him, a job that apparently she was very good at.

"We'll be opening in five months. Definitely in time for the World Series. Maybe even the playoffs."

Jacob chuckled. "Smart man. What's it going to be called again?"

"Emerald Brewing Company."

"Good name." Jacob could see Ashley attempting to stretch her arms. The cuffs were probably itching her skin at this point.

"How about I talk to Daniel, and we'll let the ladies do their Zumba at the resort. Hell, they can do it in the aerobic studio naked if they'd like. No one will see them."

Jacob ignored the tightening of his groin at Chad's suggested compromise and shook his head. Typical Whitman. Always had a quick solution that often involved some location around town. Hell, that was easy—they owned most of the businesses in it.

He continued to watch Ashley, who was now engaged in sweet talk with the intake officer, Mack, behind the counter. Dirty old man. Mack, at sixty, would cave to a pretty face, and Ashley Whitman certainly had one.

Mack and every guy in Emerald Springs, for that matter, didn't know her like Jacob did. In high school, he'd seen right through the egotistical, drama queen she was. There was, however, one incident toward the end of their senior year that he chalked up to a temporary lapse in sanity.

"Come on, Jacob." Chad slapped his back. "Beer's on me if you let her go. We can watch the Sox murder the Yankees later. I just brewed some Porch Swing last night."

That got his attention. "The beer with the pear and lime?"

"Grapefruit, ginger, and lime," Chad corrected, saying each ingredient with pride.

"That's some good shit." Jacob had never intended to arrest Ashley, but Chad's offer sealed the deal. A game and a cold beer or two tonight and catching up with his buddy sounded like a great way to start the week. "Fine. I'll write her up a warning."

"You seriously can't be ticketing me?" Ashley turned and faced him. "I was so right to turn you down in high school. Thank God I didn't go to prom with you. You deserved to go alone."

Jacob's body tensed. And there it was. The incident he'd buried so deep in the back of his mind, he thought he'd need one of his sister's bulldozers to excavate it, but Ashley had dug the painful memory out so easily with her sharp tongue. He turned and walked past her, motioning to Mack as he headed for the door. "Book her."

CHAPTER TWO

Ashley flipped on the lights to the visitor's center and rubbed her wrists, still sore where the handcuffs pinched earlier. Once Jacob stormed off, the kind officer named Mack from behind the counter had released her. He laughed the whole time and said she reminded him of a young Katherine Hepburn while slipping her his phone number and asking if she was free tonight. *Dirty old man.*

She smoothed her sleek, blonde ponytail. What a morning. All she wanted was to get an early workout in with a few friends before her Monday began and look where it got her. Now she was two hours behind. Not the best way to start out a jam-packed week.

As the marketing manager for Emerald Tea Farm, Mondays were always her busiest. She routinely spent the early part of the week in the visitor's center chatting with buyers and tourists and running the sample tea bar. A people person to her core, Ashley's favorite part of the job was interacting with the steady stream of Whitman clientele and representing the Emerald Tea brand.

She loved working on the farm and had jumped at the opportunity to be her dad's marketing assistant five years ago after graduating from the University of Portland.

Now at twenty-seven, her name had begun to generate some buzz among local business leaders.

Just last year, the Emerald Springs Chamber of Commerce had named her to its "thirty under thirty" rising stars roster, where she and the other "stars" were honored at the chamber's annual spring luncheon. That celebration with her father and extended Whitman family had been one of the best days of her life. Her dad had even purchased two tables for the event for their family and friends to celebrate her achievement. He'd been so proud, beaming all night. She knew she was starting to be taken seriously as a mover and shaker in the tea industry and not simply Sam's daughter and a Whitman heir.

Now that her cousin Adam oversaw Emerald Tea Farm, she hoped he'd soon task her with new responsibilities. The oldest of the Whitman brothers, he'd recently taken the reins from his dad—her uncle Richard. Everyone knew that Adam was being groomed to oversee the family conglomerate when Richard finally retired soon. It was a decision all the Whitmans strongly supported.

Well, maybe, not all.

Her father struggled with the fact that he now reported to Adam, a man more than half his age, who hadn't worked a day on the farm in the last fifteen years. He hadn't actually admitted that out loud, but she knew better. Just last week, she caught her dad muttering a not-so-collegial expletive under his breath about Adam.

As for her, she couldn't be more excited to have Adam in the driver's seat. He seemed genuinely eager to hear her ideas for bringing more foot traffic into the visitor's center, whereas in the past, she had to vet them through her dad, who then might or might not present them to Uncle Richard. Her cousin had made it clear to her that his office door was always open.

Adam's open door policy couldn't have come at a better time because as much as she loved all three of her cousins dearly, her competitive side wanted to give them a run for their money, proving they weren't the only Whitmans who could turn a profit.

She also secretly hoped that Daniel might let her lead new marketing campaigns for his resort. She had a real interest in spa products and cosmetics infused with tea. Sadly, that flicker of hope was snuffed when Daniel announced he'd up and married some spa chick in Australia and now she'd be his right-hand marketing director.

Ashley was dying to meet his bride and see how she would be folded in to the current marketing operation. Her dad had seemed to take the news well, even offered to help train the newest Whitman.

Powering on her laptop, she reviewed the to-do list. There just weren't enough hours in the day. In addition to her duties on the farm, last fall, she'd been invited by the International Tea Association to serve on the planning committee for the Global Tea Expo in San Diego. The annual three-day conference brought together tea industry professionals from around the world to unveil new products, conference workshops, and lots and lots of networking. Emerald Tea Farm would have a large presence at the event—it always did—where she and her dad would ably represent their products.

She cracked her neck and clicked open her calendar. Typical week. Completely filled with morning, afternoon, and evening appointments.

It didn't help her schedule that every time she turned around one of Uncle Richard's offspring was getting engaged. She'd had a hand in planning not one but two engagement parties in the last three months and was now helping Adam with his wedding. At least Daniel had eloped in Australia. She'd have to thank him for that.

Her gaze rested on her large, green conference binder she'd left on the counter last Friday. She'd be completely lying if she didn't admit there was an added bonus to planning the Tea Expo, and that bonus was tall, dark, and ever-so-handsome.

Graham Carpenter, the CEO of Seattle's Pure Tea, was chair of this year's expo. He'd been the one to personally reach out and invite Ashley to serve on the planning committee—a flattering invitation to say the least since she'd received it the day after meeting him at a networking lunch. Her father had introduced them.

She opened her "Graham" folder and smiled. It was her special place to save all of their e-mail correspondence, mostly about the Tea Expo.

But it hadn't been all work. Five months ago, they had had their first dinner at Blush Wine Bar downtown.

Graham had been back on two other occasions under the guise of conference planning. Sure, they'd worked on the expo, but the time spent together always ended in a casual dinner, talking about other things. He seemed most interested in the overnight success of Emerald Tea. She'd joked that he was her competition and she couldn't give away all their secrets.

She coiled a long strand of hair around her finger, remembering the kiss they shared the last time he was in town. It hadn't necessarily curled her toes, but Ashley knew he was a bit reserved. All signals indicated they were going in the right direction.

So she'd invited him to stay at Emerald Paradise on Saturday. With only one week to go before the expo, he was traveling back down from Seattle so they could finalize menus and volunteer assignments. Ashley had arranged a complimentary room for him at the resort, telling the reception desk that her cousin had approved it. Daniel would probably have a conniption when he learned what she did, but she'd remind him that he was her favorite cousin and all would be forgotten. Men were so easy.

If Ashley had her way—and she always got her way—she and Graham would be getting to know each other on a different level this weekend. Maybe they could enjoy one of the resort's couples spa treatments. That might really loosen him up.

She reached her phone to call the spa and see what appointments might be available but stopped. Maybe she should call Graham first and make sure he'd be up for a massage or mud bath. She swiped through her contacts until she reached his name.

He picked up immediately. "Hey, Ashley."

"Hi, Graham. Is this a good time?"

"Always a good time to hear your lovely voice. What's up?"

He likes the sound of my voice. "I'm looking forward to seeing you this weekend. Since we'll be at Emerald Paradise, I was thinking of booking spa appointments for us." She paused, not wanting to appear too eager. "If you think it might be something you'd like. Maybe a pre-conference massage … as a reward for all of our hard work. Totally up to you."

There was a pause on the other end, causing Ashley to bite down on her lip. Maybe this was a bad idea. "Of course, I don't have to make the appointments. We could … er … just work."

"No." Graham finally spoke. "That's very thoughtful of you. I think that would be a perfect way to unwind a bit before next week. Let's do it."

"Terrific." Ashley fist pumped the air. "I'll make all the arrangements."

"I'll see you Saturday then."

"See you." Ashley clicked off her phone and did a little jig. Getting the CEO in a relaxing spa room was a small victory. Would he be open to side-by-side massages? Both of their bodies slathered in oil, soft music playing in the background, flickering candlelight all around …

The doorbell's familiar chime yanked Ashley reluctantly out of her fantasy.

"Good morning, Ashley." Adam breezed in with his fiancée, Zoe Miller, by his side.

"Hello. What brings you two lovebirds in?" She grabbed her clipboard and turned to inspect the tea inventory. Since she'd lost two hours thanks to the town's deputy dog, she'd have to talk and work at the same time.

"Heard you had quite the morning." Adam snickered. "I'm thinking an orange jumpsuit would look good on you."

Ashley swiveled off her stool, determined to downplay her earlier visit to the Sheriff's department. "It was all a misunderstanding."

"Stop teasing her," Zoe said, shooting Adam a devilish smirk. She set a small, brown box on the counter that Ashley knew contained either scrumptious muffins or a breakfast cake from her bakery. She could always count on her friend for a tasty treat when she stopped by. Zoe did own the most amazing bakery in Emerald Springs.

Adam pulled up a barstool and took a seat. "So, Ash, or should I say slugger?"

"Oh, please. I barely touched him." Ashley grabbed a pitcher of iced tea and poured two glasses. "What I don't understand is why this town, let alone county, would put their trust in Jacob Sanders to protect them when he's going around wasting time harassing innocent residents. There's no way I will vote for him if he runs for sheriff." She offered a glass to Zoe. "Try this."

Zoe grabbed the tea and took a sip. "Ohhh ... I love Cherry Berry Spice."

Adam pulled her in. "Let me taste." He brushed his lips over hers.

Ashley rolled her eyes. She wasn't used to seeing her reserved, straight-laced cousin display his affection so publically.

Daniel ... maybe. Chad, definitely. But Adam ...

She reached below for forks for them to enjoy the treat. "All right, you two. Maybe you should go up to the farmhouse. I'm sure the master bedroom's available."

Adam stood. "Who says we didn't come from there?"

"Adam!" Zoe playfully punched him.

He stole one more kiss. "I'm headed to the airport at five p.m. to pick up Daniel and Rochelle. Want to join me, Ash?"

"Oh, my gosh. It's today, isn't it?" She grabbed a travel mug from behind her and filled it with iced tea for Adam. In all of this morning's brouhaha, she'd completely forgotten Daniel was coming home. "Of course. I'd love to go."

It'd be nice to have Daniel back. They'd always bonded over their sense of style and city chic sophistication. Drinking Front Porch—or whatever Chad was calling his latest brew—really wasn't her thing. She was definitely more of a Riesling type of girl who would take a Saturday night at a wine bar in Seattle anytime over watching a game at The Rusty Tap.

Ashley watched Zoe and Adam embrace. They really did look so cute together. What she wouldn't give to be in a relationship with her own Adam Whitman … just not a Whitman. She wrinkled her nose. That would be *so* wrong.

"So, Ashley." Adam chuckled. "Stay out of trouble, I'm a little light on cash," he teased, opening the door to leave.

"Very funny. Don't you have a tea farm to run?" She waved him off and settled back onto her stool to catch up with her best friend. "It's good to see you both so happy."

Zoe smiled and gave one of her infamous dreamy sighs. Ashley knew the sentence that always accompanied it.

"I can't wait to be Mrs. Adam Whitman."

Yep, that one. Ashley giggled. She'd heard it a thousand times.

"What's so funny?"

"Nothing." She motioned for Zoe to take Adam's vacated stool while she grabbed a note pad and something to write with. "Okay, so this week we're trying on your wedding and bridesmaid dresses, picking out flowers, and tasting wedding cakes." She waved her pencil in the air. "Now that Daniel's back, we can finalize the dinner menu with him and his chef this week."

"Aye-aye, captain." Zoe paused, "About the wedding cake …"

Ashley put her hands on her hips. She knew what was coming, and the answer was still no. As Zoe's maid of honor, she had to put her foot down. "Do not even say it, Zoe Miller. You are *not* baking your wedding cake. I'm sorry. I know it would be amazing, but this is your day. I've lined up some upscale bakers to come down from Seattle to do a tasting for us here on Wednesday."

"I guess that will be okay," Zoe reluctantly gave in. Ashley suspected her persistent friend would try again tomorrow. She wouldn't be Zoe if she didn't. Still, with so much to do, Ashley needed her to focus on being the bride, not a wedding cake maker.

"So let's dish, Ash." Zoe reached for her iced tea and took a sip. "What happened after Jacob hauled you off?"

"I'd rather not talk about it."

"Did they take your picture and fingerprint you?"

"No." Ashley looked down at her perfect French manicure and grimaced at the thought. "Honestly, I think it was a big joke to Jacob." Although, that wasn't exactly true. There was that moment he had stormed out of the police station in a huff. He didn't seem to be laughing then. What was his deal?

"You know, I never realized it before, but Jacob really fills out that deputy uniform rather nicely."

Ashley wiggled her nose. "Zoe! You're practically married."

"I'm just saying …"

"Well, I hadn't noticed." Jacob Sanders was the one single guy in Emerald Springs who Ashley had never considered eligible, or interesting for that matter. He'd been a jerk to her ever since Pixie White's class in second grade.

And it only escalated in high school. Asking her to the prom the way he did had been the most humiliating day of her life. She suspected his, too, but he deserved it.

Zoe continued talking, jarring Ashley's trip down memory lane. "Well, word around town is Jacob's been spending quite a lot of time with Kimi Prevost."

"Who?"

"Kimi Prevost," Zoe repeated. "You know. Colleen's husband's sister."

"Oh, right. She's the one who got caught up in the fight at Emerald Eats. That family is just weird."

"I heard Colleen's pregnant." Zoe looked down at her watch.

"Well that explains it." Ashley laughed and moved her hand up and down in a swift motion, pretending to load a revolver. "Shotgun!"

Zoe smiled. "Let's not spread that gossip. I'm still holding out hope that one day Colleen will order something from my bakery."

"Don't hold your breath. Now that you're going to be a Whitman, I'm pretty sure she'll be boycotting Everything Nice bakery, too."

"I can't wait to be a Whitman."

"You already said that." Ashley set her notepad aside with their wedding "to do" list and opened the box Zoe had brought. Inside was a mouthwatering apple crumb cake. Ashley handed Zoe a fork to share the treat. "You know. You may have snagged the last wonderful guy on the planet, or at least in Emerald Springs."

Her friend blushed. "Adam is pretty perfect, isn't he?" She raked her fork through the crumb cake. "So what about you?"

"What about me?"

"Any prospects on the horizon?"

Ashley shrugged. "No, not really."

"Then Jacob could be a contender?"

"Never going to happen. I'd rather pick every tea leaf on this farm in the hot summer heat, wearing a parka." Ashley paused. "There might be someone …"

"Who?"

"Do you want to see?" Ashley reached over and grabbed her laptop, all giddy thinking about Graham. Not wanting to jinx it, she hadn't told any of her friends that they'd kissed, not even Zoe. "I'm pretty sure his headshot is on his company website."

"Who is it?"

"Graham Carpenter."

"Who?"

"He runs a tea farm in Seattle."

Zoe raised an eyebrow. "You're dating a competitor?"

Ashley considered the last word in that sentence. It did cross her mind a time or two, but their business relationship was nothing like the one with Split Acres where Uncle Richard and Joe Sanders still avoided each other like the plague. "We don't really talk about our work—at least not much. We're both on the planning committee for the Global Tea Expo."

"Wait. You've been planning that conference for months. Why am I only hearing about him now?"

"Well, you've been kind of busy with your own love life."

"Still …" Zoe sounded hurt. She lunged for the laptop. "Let me see his picture."

"Hold on a second." Ashley opened up her browser and typed in the URL. After a couple of clicks, she spun it around. A laugh escaped her best friend's lips.

That wasn't quite the reaction Ashley had expected. Okay, maybe Graham didn't have Adam's fine bone structure, but he was definitely handsome. "What's so funny?"

"That's him?"

Ashley leaned over to double check. Maybe she'd clicked on the wrong profile. One look confirmed she had the right one. "That's him. Why are you laughing?"

"You don't see it?" Zoe pushed off of her stool, pointing to the screen.

Ashley shrugged.

"Come on. You really don't see it?"

"See what? You don't think he's cute?" A tiny amount of irritation began to creep up the back of her neck. What could possibly be so funny about this gorgeous man rocking a business suit?

"No, it's not that. He's very handsome." Zoe spun the laptop back so it faced Ashley. "And looks exactly like Jacob."

CHAPTER THREE

Jacob pulled into Split Acres Farm and shut off his ignition. Even off duty, he was allowed to drive his squad car. The sheriff's department had deemed it necessary to make him more visible to the public twenty-four seven.

With five minutes to spare, he'd arrived to pick up Kimi Prevost, Colleen's new sister-in-law. Always happy to see Kimi, he wasn't excited about where they were going. The beautiful South African bombshell was headed back to North Carolina, where she'd spent some time earlier this summer, and had asked him for a ride to the Sea-Tac airport.

He jumped out of his squad car and looked around. The farm buzzed with activity—a scene he wasn't quite used to. Colleen and her new husband, Alan Prevost, had initiated their plans to turn the once fledgling operation around.

It had been her goal all along to move away from farm-to-consumer sales, while focusing on value-added goods, selling things like apple butter and salsa online. She'd done her homework and, with Alan's backing, would be working double time to establish a national brand. They'd also be investing in floral trade and honey production. His sister had recently worked out a deal with Chad to sell him honey for his microbrewery.

Colleen was eager to try her hand at greenhouse farming, moving most of their harvest indoors. Her plans were smart, innovative, and economical.

From the looks of things, his sister and Alan were well on their way to resuscitating Split Acres, bringing new life to the farm. They evidently made a good team.

He felt the familiar twinge of guilt as he rested his eyes on the old farmhouse they'd grown up in. Not once growing up did he ever take a real interest in his farm chores, yet sometimes felt he'd cast his birthright aside. Just as his father had turned over farm operations largely to Colleen so he could follow his political ambition and run for state senator, Jacob had chosen public service, too. In college he'd chosen a different path, studying criminal justice. He enjoyed his work and took pride in the fact he contributed to the safety of Emerald Springs' citizens.

He'd never felt that pride on the farm. Not when it symbolized his father's failure compared to Richard Whitman's success.

While the Whitman kids had grown up with designer clothes and fancy wheels, Colleen and he wore second-hand clothes and had shared ownership of a beat-up truck their dad had gotten in an auction.

Things had started to turn around when their dad was elected state senator. Still, Jacob wasn't sporting a Rolex watch, the traditional graduation present Richard gave to each of the Whitmans.

Though his father and Richard Whitman avoided each other, he had no beef with any of the kids. Except for Ashley, who'd always walked around town like she owned it. He couldn't help but grin at how nice it was to put her in her place this morning.

He glanced over at the greenhouses bustling with activity. His sister could turn things around. That passion just didn't run in his blood the way it pumped through Colleen's. She was Split Acres's best chance to be seen as more than a joke in Emerald Springs.

He didn't hesitate to sell his five percent shares to Colleen when she'd asked earlier this year. It was the right thing to do. She'd dedicated her life to this place and deserved to have total control over its future and profits.

For his shares, she'd given him the acreage that bordered Split Acres and Emerald Tea Farm. He'd have the option to live on it, develop it, or lease it out. It was a good deal. For now, he decided to lease it back to his sister and brother-in-law, knowing it was a steady investment that could provide him with other backup opportunities should he not be elected sheriff in three years.

Kimi breezed out of the main office building, wheeling a large purple suitcase behind her, two oversize bags slung around both arms. "Hey, handsome."

She always knew how to put a smile on his face. "Let me help you. Is this all?" He pointed to her suitcase.

"And that one over there." She nodded behind her to where she'd left the rest of her belongings. Carlos, his sister's newest farmhand, had picked them up and was bringing them over.

"Thanks, Carlos," she said.

"You're welcome, *senorita*." He grinned and nodded to Jacob. "*Hola*, Mr. Sanders."

"Hey, Carlos." He greeted him with a quick handshake that left his hand slightly sore from the farm custodian's strong grip.

"My sister treating you well?"

"Very."

Jacob eyed the suitcases. Why did women find it imperative to travel with everything they owned? Were ten pairs of shoes really necessary?

He'd enjoyed spending time with Kimi over the last couple of weeks and was sad to see her leave. She'd been feeling like a third wheel during this visit, so Jacob was more than happy to step in and entertain her. Why not? She was single … he was single …

He'd hoped that maybe they'd take their friendship to the next level, but Kimi never seemed quite interested in going there. Sure, she flirted and appeared to enjoy having him on her arm at The Rusty Tap or at the movies, but Jacob always went home alone.

It was probably for the best. Who knew the next time she'd be back, and he certainly wasn't planning on going anywhere any time soon.

Jacob popped the trunk and lifted her luggage in, filling the entire space. "Sure you didn't forget anything?" Judging by the suitcases' weight, he highly doubted it.

"I'm ready." Kimi laughed and pointed to the closest greenhouse. "I just got back from saying goodbye to Colleen and Alan." She giggled. "I think I might have interrupted a moment."

He threw his hand up in the air, signaling her to stop. "I don't want to know." He chuckled. Although he didn't need to hear the details, it was cool to see his older sister settling down. He hadn't seen that coming—not by a long shot—didn't even know she was dating anyone and hadn't been invited to the wedding.

Still, Alan was a good guy with a strong eye for farming. It probably had something to do with his being a Prevost. They were, after all, Emerald Tea Farm's most formidable international competitor.

Maybe someday Alan and Colleen would give the Whitmans a run for their money. He smiled at the thought.

"Someone's happy." Kimi climbed into the squad car.

"Yeah." He reached for his seat belt. "Just thinking about old family rivalry."

"Ahh … the Whitmans. Are you friends with any of them?"

"Yep." He nodded. "All but one."

"Oh, really. Which one?"

"Not worth talking about." Jacob hit the gas and reversed out of the farm. He didn't need to spend the hour and a half ride to the airport talking about Ashley. He should have never let her get to him like she did earlier. He'd learned from Mack later that the old man had let her go shortly after Jacob stormed out.

"You can just drop me off at departures if you need to get back to work," she offered once they reached the airport.

"I'm off the clock." He motioned to the trunk. "Besides, you could probably use some help with those bags."

Jacob parked his car in a short-term parking lot and popped the trunk. "Shoot, Kimi. What's in here? Did you steal some of your brother's new farm tools?" he teased, lifting each suitcase to the ground.

"Would you arrest me if I did, deputy?" she asked coyly.

He pulled down the trunk lid. Now *that* would have been a wonderful use for his handcuffs.

The airport bustled with travelers, zipping past them in every direction. In no time, Kimi had picked up her ticket and checked in her luggage.

Next, she wanted to get some reading material for the long trip, so Jacob waited outside a bookstore with her carry-on belongings while she dashed inside.

He reached in his pocket and checked his phone. Hmmm, Richard Whitman had left him a cryptic voice mail message that he'd like to talk with him soon. What could that be about? The Whitmans had a serious string of bad luck recently with property damage on the farm, diner, and last month, at the resort.

One event in particular that was clearly no accident continued to weigh on his mind: Daniel Whitman's attack while jogging. Finding him on the side of the road like he did and then having him pass out in his cruiser had scared the shit out of Jacob. Maybe that's what Richard wanted to talk about. Or maybe the feds had uncovered who the imposter immigrations officials were who had visited Emerald Tea Farm earlier this summer, and he wanted to fill Jacob in. Hopefully there hadn't been another suspicious incident.

"Leaving town indefinitely, I hope?"

Jacob looked up from his phone to see the owner of the snide remark.

Ashley.

She stood in front of him wearing a sleeveless red dress, a matching clutch tucked underneath her arm.

"You'd like that, wouldn't you?" His gaze easily slid down her silky nylons to her red heels.

"Honestly, I couldn't care less." She pulled her long, blonde hair to one side. "I'm just here to pick up Daniel."

He pointed to the escalator. "Arrivals are downstairs. Try not to assault anyone."

"Worse cop ever," she mumbled and took off.

"At least I didn't peak in high school," he called out, to which she spun around and shot him a disgusted look. Had they not been in a public place he suspected her middle finger would have accompanied it. He smiled, loving the fact that this was the second time in less than twenty-four hours he'd gotten a rise out of her. God, this day kept getting better and better.

"What was that about?" Kimi asked, coming up beside him.

"Oh, nothing."

She smirked. "Ex-girlfriend?"

"God, no. She hates me."

"Hmm … didn't look like it from my vantage point."

Before he knew what was happening, Kimi latched onto his arm and dragged him across the airport. What had she meant by "from my vantage point"?

Stopping in front of the security check in, she grabbed her carry-on from Jacob. "Well, guess this is where we part." She nodded to the line of passengers.

"Guess it is." Jacob looked down at Kimi and smiled. "You have everything?"

"Sure do." She flashed her purse open and he peeked inside. It was stocked with magazines. "Six hours and a bag full of guilty pleasures. What more does a girl need?"

He chuckled. "Well, have a safe flight. Text us when you land."

She leaned in. "Don't look back, but I think we have an audience for our goodbye."

"Who?"

"The pretty blonde you were trying hard to pretend you don't like."

He turned but didn't see Ashley in the crowd. Kimi must have mistaken some other woman for her. Ashley had been heading to arrivals. She wouldn't be in this area of the airport. "You've got it all wrong. We seriously can't stand each other."

Kimi shot him a look of disbelief and then out of nowhere planted her lips on his. Jacob wrapped his arms around her, deepening the kiss without hesitation. After all, he'd been waiting for weeks to do it. It ended all too quickly as she broke contact and whispered into his ear, "You keep telling yourself that." She patted his shoulders. "I just helped you get to first base. Time to go after the girl you really want, deputy."

The girl he really wanted. Who was she talking about? Jacob jammed his fists in his pockets and watched Kimi as she winked and then disappeared deep into the security line. Scanning the crowd behind him, he caught a streak of red taking off down the escalator. Had Ashley really been watching them?

• • •

Ashley stepped out of the shower and hooked her silk crimson bathrobe. Grabbing a towel, she bent down and twisted it into a turban. It was Wednesday evening and she needed to get a move on, or she'd be late for family dinner at Emerald Eats.

The weekly event brought the whole Whitman clan together. Since she began working on the Tea Expo, she'd had to bail a time or two this spring, but tonight was also a special occasion. They were celebrating Daniel and Rochelle's marriage. Not in a million years would she miss that.

It was so nice to see her favorite cousin so deliriously in love. She reached for her cherry almond lotion and rubbed it up and down her legs. Yes, the love bug had certainly taken a gigantic bite out of Mr. "I will never get married."

When she greeted them in baggage claim, she could see instantly just how crazy Daniel was about Rochelle. The beautiful Aussie by his side brought out a new dopey grin she'd never seen on her serious cousin, and it didn't leave his face the whole ride home.

Of course, Daniel asked Ashley if he could borrow her handcuffs. For the love of God. Her cousins couldn't keep their mouths shut. Chad probably sent a group text the minute he found out that Jacob had hauled her in. The three of them were honestly worse than high school girls with their gossip.

Ashley liked Rochelle. She had a cute accent and an upbeat personality. While Adam and Daniel caught up on Whitman business, she and Rochelle had talked about Emerald Paradise. Rochelle was looking forward to rolling up her sleeves and learning all about its operation. Ashley could tell Daniel's new bride knew her stuff when it came to resort marketing.

Maybe it would be nice to have another marketing professional on the Whitman team to bounce ideas off of. Someone who wasn't her father but more of a peer.

Pulling the towel off her head, she pumped some mousse in her palm, and threaded it through her long hair. Tonight called for loose curls.

She took her time getting ready, finally selecting slim jeans and a black camisole top that showed off her tan. As she sat on her bed and slid on her black strappy heels, she knew all of her preparations for tonight were a way to distract herself from dwelling on what she'd witnessed at the airport between Jacob and Kimi Prevost.

What had possessed her to follow Jacob through the airport and then spy on him outside security? When she'd turned around at the top of the escalator and saw him talking to the strange woman, something in her just snapped. She wasn't one hundred percent sure, but it looked like Colleen's new sister-in-law, whom Ashley had seen a couple of times in Chad's diner.

Chad had mentioned in passing that Kimi and Jacob had stopped by his house to watch the game with him last week.

She'd wondered just how close the two had gotten, so she followed them.

As they appeared to be saying goodbye in front of security, Ashley ducked behind a pretzel vendor, cursing herself the entire time. She didn't even like Jacob; why would she care if he and Kimi were dating?

Then the kiss happened. She hadn't been able to pry her eyes off the couple for those few seconds, watching Jacob wrap his tan, muscular arms around Kimi.

Ashley stood and reached for her favorite white gardenia perfume on her dresser, squirting her neck and wrist. It was completely ridiculous to give the kiss a further thought since she despised him.

Who gave a flying tea leaf whom he made out with? She didn't. It was a good thing she had come to her senses and hightailed it down the escalator before Jacob caught her.

She sighed. Perhaps her obsession over the kiss was due to her missing Graham and wanting to get her lips on *him*. That had to be it. She grabbed her purse and keys off her kitchen bar. All she knew was when Graham visited this weekend, she was escalating their relationship.

The embrace Kimi and Jacob shared in the airport security line would not hold a candle to what she'd be doing with Graham at Emerald Paradise. The resort was the perfect place for a whole lot of romance. She sent him a quick text, letting him know she'd booked hot stone massages for them for Saturday afternoon. Grinning, she typed with her finger: *Don't forget to bring your swim trunks.* They'd be getting in one of Daniel's hot tubs on the property before the weekend was out.

That steamy thought kept her entertained during the ten minutes it took to drive to Emerald Eats from the west side of town. That and going over her to-do list for the morning. Adam had asked to meet with her and her father to discuss their upcoming exhibit at the Tea Expo. Uncle Richard was also invited to the meeting. She and her dad were getting together at 9:00 a.m. sharp to go over one last time the plans they'd then share with Adam and her uncle.

Her dad was anxious to get to California. He'd been talking about the expo non-stop. Ashley feared he might try to sneak out and take a trip north to see her mother, currently on husband number three, a hotshot Hollywood agent. As far as she knew, the last time they saw each other was five years ago in Portland for Ashley's college graduation. Shortly after, their divorce had been finalized.

That encounter hadn't gone well. At Ashley's celebration dinner, her tipsy dad had accused her mom of being a gold-digging tramp, whereas her mom said her father was the red-headed stepchild of the Whitmans. *Yeah, not well at all.*

Though Ashley traded e-mails and talked on the phone with her mom from time to time, they hadn't seen each other since that awful night. Ashley's allegiance had always been to her father. She would always be his little girl. When her mother left, Ashley had been there to pick up the pieces.

Her mom had broken her trust, and that was huge in Ashley's book.

Arriving at Emerald Eats, she pulled into the only available parking spot, nestling her Audi in between Chad's Jeep and Zoe's hybrid. *Looks like the gang's all here.* Hopping out, she headed in.

"Ashley! You made it." Daniel grinned, giving her a giant bear hug.

"Why wouldn't I?" She hugged him back and then slid into the empty seat between him and Zoe.

The restaurant was crowded for a Wednesday night. Everyone appeared to be there except for her uncle Richard. That was funny. She could have sworn his red truck was parked outside. At least it had the same huge dent from where Jen had backed into it a couple of months ago.

Daniel elbowed her in the ribs. "Well, we weren't sure if you were out breaking any laws."

"I knew Jacob was kidding all along," Chad joined in.

"How so?" Adam asked from his seat at the table.

"Well, Ash, did he read you your rights?" Chad asked.

Ashley shook her head. "No."

"Then it wasn't an arrest."

"What I wouldn't have done to see our Ashley in handcuffs," Daniel kidded.

"Okay, enough." She directed her order to all three Whitman cousins, who were now taking their seats with their significant others at the long table. "You've all had your fun. Let's move on."

The diner was a buzz that evening and the Whitmans contributed to the loudness, catching up and celebrating Daniel's and Rochelle's marriage.

Everyone was there including her dad, who seemed to be bending Adam's ear down at the other end of the table. No doubt about the upcoming Tea Expo. Her father was like a kid in a candy store when it came time to gloat. She hoped he wasn't taking all the credit. Most of the ideas for their interactive exhibit booth were hers, not his.

Just after the waiter took their appetizer orders, Uncle Richard finally joined them. Ashley thought he looked a bit distracted. He quickly took his seat next to Patty, the longtime Whitman housekeeper and now his girlfriend after he'd mourned Aunt Sheila's death for five years.

The Whitman clan ordered their dinner and all the talk turned to how Daniel and Rochelle met and their whirlwind courtship that led them to getting married just days ago in Australia. Daniel professed he just couldn't wait to spend the rest of his life with his soul mate as he leaned down and kissed Rochelle.

"That's my cue." Chad stood. "Ash, can you join me in the kitchen?"

"Sure, what's up?"

"Just need help with something."

She stood and followed Chad back to the kitchen where two trays full of champagne flutes greeted them. Giggling, she picked up one of the glasses and inspected it. "I was hoping this wouldn't be a dry dinner."

"Not on your life. Try it and make sure it tastes all right."

Ashley brought the flute to her lips and took a sip. She could instantly taste the green tea infused with the bubbly. "Very nice." She took a longer drink. "Just the right amount of tea. Good job."

"Phew. Wasn't sure I could pull off Dad's signature drink."

"Well you did." She took another sip and looked out the kitchen back at the table. Everyone was having such a good time. Her gaze zoomed over to the entrance, and her stomach began to churn. She glared at the buzzkill that just walked in. "I wonder what he's doing here?" She set her glass down.

Chad peered over her shoulder. "Jacob's been dropping in for dinner a lot lately." He squeezed her shoulders. "I doubt he's here to arrest you, but if you want to hide in the freezer …"

"Very funny." She watched as her uncle Richard greeted Jacob, patting him on the back. She cocked her head. "What do you think that's about?"

Chad shrugged.

"You don't think it has anything to do with what Jacob did to me on Monday, do you?"

"No, I doubt it. Dad wanted to talk to him about some things."

"Some things?" she asked, raising a curious eyebrow. "Like what?"

All of a sudden, Jacob turned and caught her gaze. He smirked. *Oh, God. He knows I was spying on him at the airport*. No, that can't be. She tried to rationalize. He couldn't possibly have seen her with his lips glued to Kimi's like they were. But what if he did? What would she say? Turning away, she grabbed her flute and tilted the stem all the way up.

"Might want to go easy tonight." Chad handed the champagne tray to a waitress, instructing her to start by serving the special pink flute to the bride and then the rest to the family. Then he asked a second waitress to bring dessert out in about forty minutes.

Ashley followed Chad back to the table. The glance between her and Jacob a minute ago was nothing compared to the stare down as she passed him to take her seat. Their arms touched slightly and Ashley's heart began to beat fast. She sat down and raked her fingers through her curls, trying to ignore the tingling sensation spreading over her entire arm.

Jacob said goodbye to the family and headed to the restaurant's bar counter while Ashley reached for a new champagne glass.

Zoe leaned in. "I saw that."

"Saw what?" She tilted her glass back. Screw waiting for the toast. Knowing Adam, he'd probably deliver it and go on and on like he did at Chad's engagement party.

"Um … you purposely brushed his arm." Zoe smirked.

"Please. You're delusional." She rolled her eyes but could tell her best friend wasn't buying it.

Ashley tried to not look behind her, concentrating on the dinner conversations. She apparently wasn't the only one enjoying the bubbly. Her dad boasted loudly about the upcoming Tea Expo. Uncle Richard seemed to take a keen interest in hearing all the details and how exactly Emerald Tea would be represented. He said he was very proud and that he couldn't wait to see the exhibit plans tomorrow.

As Uncle Richard and Adam delivered their toasts, Ashley smiled, taking it all in.

It was nice to have all the family together along with these new additions. Zoe, Jen, and now Rochelle seemed to fit in just perfectly with the Whitman clan.

Wouldn't it be great if she had someone to contribute to the family's growth spurt? Could Graham be that guy?

She looked down at her flute. Once again she was somehow late to the party. While her cousins seemed to be constantly moving forward with both their professional and personal lives, she was always one step behind.

Maybe Jacob was right. Maybe she did peak in high school. There she had been popular, well liked, and had been voted most likely to succeed. She glanced over at her dad. Would she ever be seen as a major player in Emerald Tea Farm under his wing? She wasn't quite confident the answer was yes.

As everyone finished their dinner, a waitress came over carrying a round white cake decorated with an edible emerald green bow.

"Chad, is that from my bakery?" Zoe asked.

"Maybe …" He grinned and motioned for the waitress to set it down in front of Daniel and Rochelle. "I had Courtney whip it up just for tonight."

Ashley studied Chad. Why would he ask Zoe's assistant to bake a cake without telling Zoe? He was hiding something. The look he exchanged with Daniel was a dead giveaway.

Daniel slid the cake over to his dad. "Why don't you cut it for us?" He handed him the cake knife the waitress had also brought out.

"Okay." Uncle Richard sliced into the bow's rich frosting, stopping halfway through. "What the …" Continuing to maneuver his knife inside, he pulled out a miniature baby doll covered in frosting. "What is this?"

Ashley gasped. "Oh, my God. Are you—"

Daniel beamed. "The green ribbon is in honor of the newest Whitman." He reached down and touched Rochelle's stomach. "We're having a baby."

Uncle Richard's eyes watered, overcome by the realization he was going to be a grandfather. He and Daniel embraced, and then all of the table stood and congratulated the newlyweds.

Ashley hugged both of them. "I'm so happy for you both." She chuckled. "Nice touch with the emerald green bow. I should have known it represented our family."

Daniel squeezed her back. "I learned special touches from the best." He leaned in. "Who knows. Maybe your celebration will be next."

Ashley bit down on her lip. She glanced behind her at the diner's counter and saw Jacob watching the game. Two women she didn't recognize were on each side of him, clearly vying for his attention. She turned around. "Maybe. It is my turn, I suppose."

Adam came up between the two and gave his brother a big hug. "And you said marriage wasn't for you."

Daniel laughed. "I just wanted to do something in life before *you*," he kidded.

As the evening's merriment began to wind down, Ashley excused herself from the table to use the restroom, humming to herself down the corridor. She wasn't watching where she was going and slammed into something hard.

Strike that, someone hard.

"Looks like you're celebrating." Jacob grinned, not moving from where they had collided.

Ashley stepped back, nearly taking out one of Chad's team baseball pictures that hung on the wall. She attempted to regain her composure. "Yes, we are. That's what normal families do."

Ouch, Ashley. She realized that was a low blow. Maybe he and Colleen had Sunday dinners together. How would she know?

"Must be hard for you." He nodded toward the Whitman table.

"What must be hard?"

He shrugged. "Engagements, marriages, babies, happily ever afters." He paused. "What do you think you're doing wrong?"

Jerk. He deserved the crack she made. She squared her shoulders. "As a matter of fact, I have a boyfriend." She realized that was a stretch—okay, a lie, but Jacob didn't need to know that. "Not that it is any of your business, but he's coming here on Saturday."

"He doesn't live in Emerald Springs?"

"No. Seattle," she said confidently. "We're getting ready for a trip to San Diego."

"I see ..." Jacob reached behind her, his masculine cologne filling her lungs, causing her knees to shake.

She glanced up to see him fixing the photo she had knocked off its center. "See what?" she croaked, trying to ignore that all it would take was one motion from him and his arms would be down and around her.

"How you'd be attractive from ninety miles away."

Ashley's jaw dropped. He turned and strolled out the diner without even a backward glance.

Part of her wanted to run out and give him a piece of her mind, but a bigger part wanted to soak up the spicy, earthy scent he'd left in his wake. Something she could do without him, Zoe, or any of her cousins knowing about it.

That part won out. She leaned back on the wall and took a deep breath, scolding herself for allowing her enemy's delicious scent to leave her intoxicated.

CHAPTER FOUR

Jacob sat across from Richard and folded his arms. The senior Whitman had cornered him in the parking lot at Emerald Eats earlier in the week and asked to meet him at Emerald Paradise.

It was now Saturday, and he was off duty. Richard had insisted they needed to talk—"off the record."

He was meeting Richard for breakfast, which seemed a little odd to Jacob since the resort's restaurant was currently closed due to last month's water pipe burst that destroyed the kitchen.

Richard had greeted Jacob in the lobby and escorted him to an empty meeting room a few steps from the lobby.

"I thought we should meet in private this morning," Richard said and took a seat.

"Good idea." Jacob followed suit and set his notepad down, while clicking on his pen.

One of Daniel's staff immediately appeared with coffee and a basket full of muffins.

Richard grabbed the basket. Tilting it, he let Jacob pick first. "Zoe's been keeping us stocked with these delicious morsels while the kitchen is closed." He laughed, adding, "Personally, I wish we sold her baked goods all the time. My future daughter-in-law sure knows how to make them."

Jacob selected a blueberry muffin, bit down, and agreed. He reached for his coffee, grateful they didn't offer him tea. He'd never had a taste for the drink. Honestly, he couldn't quite understand how the Whitmans made a fortune off of it. A fact that, to this day, still made his father twitch. Yet, here he was having breakfast with arguably one of the wealthiest farmers in the industry.

"So, what exactly would you like me to do for you, Mr. Whitman?"

"Please call me Richard."

"Okay, Richard." Jacob felt a little uncomfortable addressing him by his first name. The old man across from him had always been Mr. Whitman as far back as he could remember.

"Look, I know what I'm about to suggest will probably sound like I've jumped off the deep end. Believe me. I thought maybe I had, too, but I can't shake off this feeling that these events are more than random accidents. Not after what happened to Daniel."

"Has Daniel remembered anything else about the night he was jumped?"

"Yes."

Jacob leaned in, choosing his words wisely. He didn't want to upset the senior Whitman.

"Is there anything else I should know?"

Richard nodded. "Daniel left out one important fact."

"Which was?" Jacob's body tensed as Richard buttered his muffin, taking his sweet old time answering the question. What kind of games were the Whitmans playing, holding this evidence from law enforcement? While he never understood why his father held onto his grudge with the family for as long as he had, this "above the law" behavior wasn't going to be tolerated. Hell no. Not on his watch.

Richard rose and shut the door. "The man who attacked my son told Daniel the hit had been a warning."

Jacob's grip on his pen tightened. "Why would Daniel keep that a secret?"

"Because my boys and I agreed that I should be the one to talk to you. Listen, Jacob." Richard leaned in. "Someone is going to great lengths to bring my empire down. I need to know who, and I need this handled with discretion."

Jacob folded his arms. He wouldn't exactly call the Whitman properties an empire. Successful, yes. "So you think hiding this information from the sheriff's department was a smart move?"

"Yes." He paused, appearing to be conflicted by the answer. "No, I knew what I asked Daniel to do was wrong, but I was afraid it would leak to the media. I wanted the dust to settle for a couple of weeks before I talked to you."

Jacob studied Richard. He understood the man's desire not only to protect his family but also the Whitman brand, but who were any of them to hold back this information? "So you think Daniel's attack was intentional?"

"I do, and I think it's related to all the other string of events happening on our properties. Someone has set out to purposely attack my legacy."

Jacob sipped his coffee. It was true that there had been several odd incidents over the last six months; the first one involving immigration imposters snooping in Richard's records had been turned over to the feds. As far as he knew, it was still under investigation.

He and the sheriff had multiple conversations about the possibility that the fire at Emerald Eats and the pipes bursting at Emerald Paradise might have been intentional, but the proof just wasn't there. "Do you have an idea who might be doing this?"

"No clue." He shrugged and then narrowed his eyes. "I want you to know that I don't suspect Joe."

Jacob couldn't help but snicker. His father might be impulsive, opinionated, and quick with his tongue, but he'd never hurt anyone, not even his oldest rival. "Sir, it's definitely not my dad." He paused not quite sure he should share this next bit of news, but it would prove to Richard his father wasn't involved. "There've been some incidents at Split Acres as well."

"Incidents?"

"Tampered crops, faltered wiring, and the deliberate pouring of cement in my sister's truck."

"When?"

"Over the last couple of months."

Richard hit the table with his fist. "Who is out to get us, and why are they attacking Emerald Tea Farm and Split Acres? That makes no sense."

Richard's last sentence stung Jacob's pride a bit. Everyone in town knew that Split Acres barely turned a profit on a good year. "That seems to be the question, doesn't it? Is there anyone who you and dad worked with in the past that comes to mind? A disgruntled employee from WhitSand Farm, maybe?"

"Son, that was twenty years ago. Joe and I pissed off plenty of people back in the day. That's the nature of farming and being involved in the community. We squared off with half the town regarding zoning rights." He rubbed his chin in thought. "I can't think of anyone who would intentionally want to destroy us."

Jacob shifted in his chair. "I'm going to need Daniel to come down to the sheriff's department and give another statement."

"He's not going to be in any trouble, is he?"

"No, I'll explain everything to the sheriff. If these incidents are connected, we need to re-examine all of the evidence." He paused, exercising his law enforcement authority. "And that means Daniel coming in and giving another statement."

"He will. Thank you, Jacob."

"You're welcome." Jacob stood but Richard motioned for him to stay seated. "Something else I can do for you?"

"I have a hunch where the bastard might strike next."

Man, Richard was certainly playing Perry Mason. Regardless, Jacob needed to hear him out in case there was any merit to his hunch. "Where?"

"Next week is the Global Tea Expo. It's in San Diego this year, and we have a huge presence in it."

San Diego. Where had he heard that city mentioned recently? He straightened in his chair, remembering immediately who was going to San Diego. *Ashley.*

"You really think the next incident will take place at the conference?"

Richard nodded. "Yes."

"In San Diego?"

"It makes sense. All of our properties have been sabotaged. Why wouldn't the perpetrator focus on the largest event that puts Emerald Tea in the global spotlight?"

He had a point, although Jacob still thought it was a bit of a stretch. "And will all of you be at the expo?" He already knew Ashley and her Seattle boyfriend were headed down.

Richard shook his head. "I don't think we should. If we all go and I'm wrong, something could happen here. I've asked Adam to skip it and have Sam and Ashley represent us. They were planning on being there anyway, so it won't raise suspicion."

He continued, his voice lighter, "Although, I'd rather keep my brother here where I can keep an eye on him. He's a bit of a loose cannon in public. Never know what kind of message he's delivering to attendees." He laughed. "But that's another story."

"So how can I help?" Jacob finished his muffin and crinkled up the wrapper, wondering if it would be totally inappropriate to grab another. They were so good.

"I want you to accompany them," Richard said firmly.

"You want me to go to the expo with Sam and Ashley?" That got more than a curious eyebrow out of him.

"Yes."

"As what? Their bodyguard?" He paused, realizing that sounded a bit rude. "I mean no disrespect, Mr. Whitman."

"Richard."

"Richard," he repeated.

"Listen, Jacob. I want you there to keep an eye on the exhibit they're planning to set up. See if anything happens to it during the expo." He leaned forward. "Keep an eye on its activity. See if anyone lingers around a little too long or takes more of an interest than they should."

"And you don't think sending law enforcement there will raise suspicion?" he asked skeptically.

"Not if you're undercover. There are thousands of attendees. I'll pay you triple what the sheriff is paying you." He paused. "Bottom line, I need someone I trust not only to guard the exhibit but more importantly to keep an eye on Ashley and Sam. I don't want either of them in a situation like Daniel was in. Who knows what this asshole would be willing to do next. If you think it's too much to keep tabs on both of them, I'll keep Sam here. Will you do this for me, Jacob?"

Jacob rested his arm on the back of the chair, contemplating Richard's request. If these activities weren't accidents and had a more sinister intent, he should look closer at the evidence they'd collected.

But did he need to go to San Diego? Surely he'd be able to arrange for the city's local law enforcement to assist?

Could he really spend three days shadowing Ashley? Would she even let him? That was probably the better question. "Can I think about it?"

Richard nodded. "But not for long. The expo starts on Thursday. Ashley leaves on Tuesday and Sam gets in two days later. I'll have Adam's assistant make all of your arrangements."

Jacob finished his coffee. So he'd have to spend nearly a week with Ashley and a couple of days alone with her before her father arrived. He folded his arms. The situation was serious, but he couldn't help but grin. "You know your niece isn't going to like this. She's not my biggest fan."

Richard returned the grin. "I heard you two had a run-in."

"Something like that." He shrugged.

"I'll have Adam talk to her. She'll be on her best behavior." He winked, adding, "You better be, too."

Jacob shifted uncomfortably at the insinuation.

A few minutes later they wrapped up their conversation with Jacob promising he'd have a decision by tomorrow morning, although the ball really wasn't in his court. He suspected the persistent Whitman wasn't going to accept any answer but yes.

Daniel appeared at that moment to greet them. "Hey, Dad. Hey, Jacob. Everything good?"

"Hey, son." Richard leaned in. "I've told Jacob our hunch on all the odd things going on around here. You'll need to go down to the station and make another statement."

Daniel shifted on his feet. "I can come anytime."

"Thanks, man," Jacob said. "Let's plan on you coming in on Monday morning. I'll let the sheriff know you've remembered something else." The Whitmans so owed him for this. He turned to Richard. "Next time, let us do our jobs."

"Let's hope there isn't a next time," Richard said, turning to Daniel. "Working today, son?"

"Every day until my expansion plans are a reality." Daniel grinned at his father. "Care to stick around and let my staff give you a men's facial before you leave? My top estheticians can take you right now."

Richard let out a chuckle. "No, I don't think so. Patty and I have plans to have lunch with Adam and Zoe and then do some gardening."

Daniel rolled his eyes. "Excuses. Excuses." He glanced down at Jacob. "How about you, deputy?"

Jacob pushed his chair back, uncomfortable with the direction the conversation had taken. Daniel was offering him a facial? He didn't really know what that entailed, but it sounded way too girly. Definitely his cue to leave. "No, I don't think so."

"Come on." Daniel slapped Jacob's back. "It's on me. Claudia up front will get you checked in. Look, man, you'd be doing me a favor. I'm trying to decide if we should offer this service. Rochelle says it's very popular in Australia, but I'm not convinced American dudes will like it."

"Why don't you ask Chad?" Jacob stood and searched his pocket for his car keys.

"I would, but he and Jen are off zip-lining, or rock climbing, or something."

Jacob laughed. He loved that his buddy had found his match when it came to the outdoors. He and Jen seemed like a perfect pair.

Daniel stood in the doorway and motioned to the front desk. "You do it, and I'll throw in a complimentary mud bath." A young, dark-haired woman appeared. "Hey, Claudia. This special client is going to do a men's facial today for us. Can you get him checked in and escort him to the treatment room?"

Claudia smiled up at Jacob, showing off cute dimples. "Wonderful! Right this way."

"Also, put him in the mud bath after the facial." Daniel turned to Jacob. "Trust me, buddy. You're going to love it." He leaned in so only Jacob could hear. "And if there's anyone you'd like to invite to the resort to join you in the mud bath, just tell the reception desk her first name. They'll show her where to go."

Jacob smirked. He wished Daniel had issued this invitation last week before Kimi flew to the other side of the country. Although, truth be told, he was kind of surprised how he'd felt after their lip lock. Though the South African beauty knew how to kiss, it didn't leave him wanting more like he thought it would.

He hated to admit it, but the tiny little act of reaching up and fixing that damn crooked picture behind Ashley in the back hallway of Emerald Eats had aroused him way more.

He shrugged off the thought. The last thing he needed to do was start thinking about Ashley Whitman in arousing terms. Maybe an afternoon here would clear his mind to focus on what Richard had suggested—that something more deliberate was happening to the Whitmans.

Besides, the mud bath sounded awesome as hell, even if he'd be alone in it. "Fine. I'll do it."

"Fabulous. My staff will take good care of you."

"Yeah, yeah, whatever. This stays here, got it?" If any of his buddies from the station found out that he'd spent his day off at Emerald Paradise getting a facial, he'd never hear the end of it. He followed Claudia to the treatment room.

"Have fun Ashley," Daniel joked.

Jacob didn't need to turn back to know Daniel was probably laughing his ass off.

• • •

Ashley pulled into Emerald Paradise and parked in her usual spot. She could hardly wait a single second longer to see Graham. He'd texted her earlier that he was thirty minutes away, but then she'd got carried away trying to decide on the perfect outfit. Before she knew it, an hour had passed. He must be at the resort by now.

Pulling down her visor, she checked her appearance. Yep, her makeup was flawless.

She'd been experimenting with a new lip gloss made with tea that plumped her lips. One day, she'd love to own a new line of tea-infused beauty products that maybe resorts like Daniel's would carry. Earlier this year, she'd found a startup company in Olympia that was blending some foundations for her using Emerald's green tea.

She even had a name for her future line: "A Touch of Ash," and in the line she'd offer BeauTEA—Emerald Tea-infused products.

She reached in her backseat and grabbed her conference binder. She'd asked Graham to meet her in the enclosed patio. They could work for a couple of hours and then maybe take their work outside to the beautiful manicured garden that overlooked the lake ... or maybe Graham's villa, if he suggested it.

Had it really been more than a month since she had a spa treatment? Her body was begging to skip the conference work and go straight for the massage.

She entered the lobby and slid up to the front desk, not recognizing the woman behind it. Must be a new employee. "Hi, I'm Ashley Whitman."

"Claudia Jones."

"Nice to meet you. When did you start, Claudia?"

"Just moved to Emerald Springs last week."

"That's awesome. Welcome, I'm sure you will love it here." Ashley set her oversized, black hobo bag on the counter. "Can you tell me if Graham Carpenter has arrived?"

Claudia punched her computer keys. "No, not yet."

"That's strange." Ashley looked out the window but couldn't see the parking area. She hadn't thought to look for his car when she drove in. "I thought he'd be here by now."

"Maybe he's here but hasn't checked in. What does he look like?"

Ashley smiled. "You can't miss him. Talk, dark, so handsome."

Claudia's face lit up. "Oh, he's here. He just finished with a facial and is in the mud room."

"Really?" Ashley cocked an eyebrow. That was a surprise. Perhaps it was a spur-of-the-moment kind of thing. Since when did Daniel offer men's facials, anyway?

"Yes." Claudia looked down at her watch. "His facial should have wrapped up twenty minutes ago. He's definitely in there."

Ashley turned her back to the counter. So a very relaxed and naked Graham was in the candlelit mud room ... alone. The devil in Ashley stepped onto her shoulder and approved the idea that popped into her head. She spun around. "Claudia, can you block that room for the next two hours?"

Ten minutes later, Ashley tiptoed into the dark mudroom and smiled. Sure enough, the only light came from the few candles spread throughout. Graham's back was to her and he appeared to be hunched over with his head resting on his arms.

Poor baby. She knew how hard he'd been working on the expo. Her own contribution was only a fraction of the time he put into it.

She could see tiny earphones coming from his ears. All of his body, including his short dark hair, was completely covered in mud.

Slipping out of the resort's comfy, white bathrobe, she stepped into the tub. She would have preferred to go in naked, but didn't want to completely freak Graham out if, by some off chance, he didn't respond the way she'd hoped. She'd put on a bikini she kept in her locker when sun bathing at the resort.

It would probably be ruined from the mud, but this occasion was so well worth it.

She took in his hot body for a second: long, muscular, and so needing to be touched. A Blake Shelton song was coming out from his earbuds. Awesome. A bonus that he liked country music as it was her favorite, too. The more she learned about his interests, the more she knew they were well-suited for each other.

She waded over, letting the green tea-infused mud saturate her skin. The warm grains immediately relaxed her. It had always been her favorite treatment, and somehow being in here in the romantic candlelight with an unsuspecting Graham made it that much more fun. She snuck up behind him and placed her hands on his shoulders and began to rub. Needling his neck, she grabbed a handful of mud and exfoliated his back.

Wow. She knew he had a dark tan from working in his tea fields, but his shoulders were so broad and muscular. She hadn't realized this. His business suits always made him appear a little on the lanky side, but he was, without a doubt, solid. A definite bonus. Now all he needed to do was turn around and wrap his tight biceps around her.

Without saying a word, he cocked his head to the side, which she took as a nonverbal approval to her teasing his pressure points. If this was what he liked, she'd happily oblige. "Just thought you could use some help," she breathed and swirled some of the mud across his back. "You know green tea mud is very arou—"

"Ashley?" She turned around and her mouth flew open.

Standing in front of her was Graham. Dressed in a black business suit, lanky arms and all.

She pushed back. "What the hell?"

The mud-caked stranger she'd just rubbed down turned around and pulled out his earbuds. "*Jacob?*"

This wasn't happening.

"I think I'll leave you two alone." Graham turned to leave.

"Wait! You have this all wrong." Ashley attempted to get out of the tub. She slipped and fell face first into the mud. Jacob's muddy hands went immediately to her waist, pulling her up.

She fought to free herself from him and regain her composure. "Don't touch me," she yelled. "Graham, I can explain."

"I'll be at the coffee bar working." He exited, and Ashley turned to Jacob, ready to let him have it.

He inched closer, his mud-crusted chest looking just as inviting as his back had. Any verbal combat she planned to launch had decided to ignore her orders and ceased fire.

Jacob touched her cheek with the back of his hand, flinging some mud away. That single stroke sent a shiver down her spine.

He leaned in and her mouth parted. Ashley's inner voice sent her a blaring warning message.

Enemy's lips approaching. Move the hell back.

She ignored it.

Her gaze rested on the candle flames flickering over his beautiful, full lips. She really should be chasing after Graham, not waiting for Jacob's mouth to press up against hers. But for reasons she couldn't explain, there was no place she'd rather be.

Jacob moved his mouth to her ear. "Thanks for the back rub. You should probably go talk to your boyfriend." He turned and stepped out of the tub, giving her full view of his naked backside before disappearing into the adjoining shower.

CHAPTER FIVE

Jacob sat at the bar in The Rusty Tap and downed his beer. The cold mixture coated his throat, hitting the spot. As far as days went, today had been one of the strangest and definitely called for one or two cold ones to help process it all.

What the hell had happened in the spa? One minute he was feeling the most relaxed he'd ever felt, enjoying the mud bath while listening to a little country music. The next, his dick was hard and ready for some action, courtesy of the last woman on earth he thought he'd ever be naked with.

He couldn't shake the image of Ashley's freakin' hot body covered in mud. Even before he knew it was her, there was something about the way she'd massaged his back that had sent a sensation he'd never experienced before through him.

At the time, he thought Daniel had sent in one of his staff to throw in the little bonus massage. He didn't know how these spa treatments worked.

When he realized it was Ashley who was responsible for his arousal, all he wanted was to scoop her up and completely devour her right then and there. How did the one woman he despised in this town stir this desire within him? Ever since he'd hauled her into the station on Monday, these new feelings were starting to seriously mess with his head.

He took another sip of his beer. Who was he kidding? Shit. If he was completely honest, those feelings were not new. Far from it. They'd just been buried for quite some time.

For years, he and Ashley had gone about their lives, hardly saying a word—and certainly not a kind one—to each other. For his part, he knew his sharp tongue was the result of always feeling he wasn't good enough for the beautiful Whitman.

Ashley had never liked him. Before their families began feuding, Jacob and Colleen had spent hours at the Whitman farmhouse playing imaginary games with all the kids. Ashley always cast him as the bad guy. Even at eight, she'd put him in his place.

He shook his head. Why had the universe thrown them together this week—the station, the airport, the diner, the spa … was this some kind of joke?

And why the hell had she mistaken him for her douche bag boyfriend? Seriously? From what he could tell they looked nothing alike. Jacob hadn't been in a suit and tie since his dad's senate inauguration.

Still, the sheer horror on her face when she realized it was he and not Graham in the mud bath was priceless. Never in his wildest imagination did he ever think he'd be touching Ashley, but there he was … hands on her waist. Okay, maybe he was only saving her from drowning in mud, but when he had gotten closer, all he could think about was how much he wanted to kiss her.

She'd wanted it, too, which had totally surprised him. The way she'd gazed at him with her lips parted—it wasn't just the warm mud causing the heat between them.

If he had gone for it and taken possession of her lips, she would have kissed him back. She might have slapped him after the fact to save face, but she wouldn't have turned away. He was sure of it.

Still, she had a boyfriend, who, not to forget, caught her with her hands all over another guy. Not a situation Jacob wanted to get in the middle of. It was probably better that she was already taken. Ashley Whitman wasn't the woman for him. Those old feelings would just need to go back to the deep corner of his mind where they belonged.

He'd done the right thing jumping out of the mud bath when he did. He took a shower—a cold one—and then left the resort without another run-in.

He eyed the baseball game playing while mulling over Richard's request. No way was he going to San Diego. Ashley's boyfriend could look after her. Jacob could talk to law enforcement there and perhaps see if someone local could keep an eye on her and her father. Maybe he could arrange for a police officer to stop by and check in with them each morning.

He'd make some calls tomorrow and see who could help him. Then he'd let Richard know the plan. The senior Whitman might not be happy with him, but it just didn't make sense for Jacob to take time off to explore a theory that bordered on paranoia.

If on the off chance Richard was right, wouldn't it make more sense for another suspicious event to happen here in Emerald Springs, not at a global tea conference where there were thousands of witnesses?

Although he wouldn't be going to San Diego, he'd talk to his boss about taking another hard look at all the evidence. That might appease Richard. Perhaps they'd uncover something they hadn't originally seen. Richard was right, the phony immigration officials were definitely no accident, but that incident had been turned over to the feds months ago.

Yet there was the matter of suspicious activity his sister experienced earlier this spring as well. Colleen hadn't reported anything recently, but if Richard was right, someone could be causing trouble for both the Whitmans and his family.

But why? Who would want to mess with both Emerald Tea Farm and Split Acres? Everyone knew it was going to take a lot for Colleen and Alan to get the farm in the black again. To think that the incidents were related didn't make sense.

He grabbed his phone from the bar and checked the time. It was getting late, and he'd planned to help Colleen and Alan in the greenhouses in the morning. It was going to be nice to hang out with his sister and new brother-in-law.

Standing, he reached in his back pocket for his wallet. For a Saturday night, the bar was surprisingly empty. He glanced out the window, noticing two men greeting on the sidewalk.

"What the hell?" Jacob sat back down and turned his head. He didn't want to be obvious, but he needed to get a better look at the two men who now appeared to be in conversation.

Why was Ashley's boyfriend talking to his sister's hired hand? He watched as Graham handed a dark folder to Carlos, who quickly tucked it into his chest and zipped up his black leather jacket.

Well, wasn't that interesting? He ordered another beer and continued to watch the men talk. A few minutes later, they appeared to be done with their conversation and took off in opposite directions down Spruce Street.

Jacob took a sip of his mug. It looked like he'd be taking a trip to San Diego after all.

• • •

Ashley sucked in her breath and took a seat in the second floor conference room. She and her father had just finished reviewing their detailed agenda for the Tea Expo with Adam and Uncle Richard.

Even though her nerves jittered on the inside, on the outside she was poised and confident. After all, she'd worked months on this conference. Adam and Uncle Richard seemed impressed and had acknowledged her hard work several times. Both were pleased with the activities she and her dad had put together for attendees to learn more about Emerald Tea Farm's selection and sample their popular blends. They even planned a contest exclusive to attendees to name a fall tea.

Her dad had sat back and let her take the lead.

Through a partnership with a local beauty school in San Diego, Ashley had arranged for some of the students to offer mini-facials and massages all weekend, using some of the tea-infused products Daniel sold at the resort. Finally, they'd offer drawings every hour for cool tea-inspired prizes with the grand prize a week's stay at Emerald Paradise.

Uncle Richard hadn't asked many questions during their meeting but had lit up during Ashley's idea of the tea-naming contest and the added promotion for the spa. "You two have done a wonderful job," Adam began.

"We really have," her dad boasted. "It's going to be a great exhibit, probably our best showing ever. I can't wait to get down there."

"Actually, Uncle Sam, there's been a change in plans." Adam swiveled his chair toward Ashley. "I want Ashley to represent us. Alone."

Ashley's mouth flew open, but she quickly shut it. Had she heard her cousin correctly?

"You can't pull me off this," her dad sneered. "I always go. It's the biggest marketing event for Emerald Tea." He turned to Uncle Richard. "Can I speak to you in private?"

"You can, but I support Adam's decision. Sam, there's too much going on here with all of these accidents that seem to plague the family. I need you to help us climb out of this PR nightmare."

Her dad shook his head. "I've already booked my flight and hotel. Besides, there hasn't been an incident in almost a month."

Uncle Richard dismissed his attempts. "Sam, we've made our decision. You'll go next year. Isn't it in London? You'll like that one."

Ashley sat quietly as her dad and uncle went at it. She'd just been given the golden ticket she'd been waiting for: the opportunity to shine and prove her value to this family. She watched as her dad followed Uncle Richard out of the conference room. It was unlikely her father would lie down and play dead without a fight.

It would be a fight he'd most likely lose, and she was more than confident she'd be fine without him. She loved her dad, but truth be told, she was itching to go it alone and prove she could handle it.

A small part of her also wanted to keep him out of California so as to avoid any temptation he might have to visit her mother while there. It would be just like him to rent a car and disappear up the coast for a day or two. He didn't need that heartache.

Adam stood and touched her shoulder. "You okay with this?"

"Yes, absolutely." She crossed her legs and pushed up her wire-rimmed glasses. Running late this morning, she hadn't had time to put her contacts in. "I'm just surprised you'd cancel his trip at this late hour."

"Dad has his reasons." He smiled and pointed to the agenda she'd passed out earlier. "And he has all the confidence in the world that you will do a wonderful job representing us this year. I agree."

"Thank you. I won't let you down. I just don't know how dad's going to take it. I'm sure my phone will be ringing nonstop."

"We'll keep him busy here." He winked, adding, "And out of your hair."

She sighed and gazed out the window. "It's probably for the better that he skips this one. I had a sneaky suspicion that he'd use the opportunity of being in California to drive up and see my mother."

"How's Aunt Elizabeth doing?"

Ashley shrugged. "Same. You know, loves to party and spend her new husband's money." She didn't really want to talk about her mother, so she changed the subject back to the issue at hand. "If you need my dad here to help with PR, are things really that bad?"

"No. Not really. Dad's got some ideas of what may be going on."

"Going on?"

"With the diner and resort. This doesn't leave this room, but he's not convinced either was an accident."

She raised an eyebrow. "What about the farm's broken fence? Does he think someone purposely tore it down to compromise our organic status?"

"Yes." He sighed. "He does."

"Wow."

"Then there's what happened to Daniel."

Ashley's eyes widened. "You think Daniel's assault is related somehow?"

"It's possible."

"Why is this happening?" The thought that someone was deliberately out to get the family sent a blow to her gut. Didn't this only happen on the Lifetime TV Network? "It's only a hunch. We have no proof," Adam was quick to add. "Dad wants Uncle Sam to stay here to help me with our public image."

She stood and gathered her things, satisfied with his answer. "I guess I'm going to San Diego alone then."

Adam raked his hair with his hand. "Ash, about that …"

"What?"

"Well … you're not exactly going to be there by yourself."

"I'm not?" Was Chad or Daniel going?

Adam motioned to her chair. "You might want to sit down for this."

CHAPTER SIX

Ashley sat down, shoved her black tote bag underneath the seat in front of her, and latched her belt buckle around her waist.

"Nervous?"

She peered over at Graham sitting next to her in a suit and tie. After picking him up at his house at an ungodly hour, they were finally settling in for their three hour flight to San Diego.

"Not really. I love to fly." She cocked her head and glanced down the aisle. No. Flying nerves weren't the cause of her edginess. The hairs on the back of her neck rose as she watched Jacob take his seat toward the front of the plane.

Why Adam and Uncle Richard had insisted that the bane of her existence attend the Tea Expo, she didn't understand. For God's sake, he nearly threw her into the slammer just last Monday and now he was her assigned protection? In what universe was this a good idea? Certainly not hers.

She didn't need protecting and certainly not by him.

Adam had patiently listened to her rant and then attempted to calm her down. He explained that Uncle Richard had personally asked Jacob to join her just as a precaution. They didn't really expect anything bad to happen at the expo, but on the off chance that something did, Jacob would be there to step in.

Uncle Richard trusted Jacob, and Ashley knew from firsthand experience that once his mind was made up, there was no changing it. She'd watched her dad lose that battle yesterday.

Apparently that's why Jacob had been at Emerald Paradise. He'd been meeting with her uncle to discuss his new chaperoning gig.

Like it or not, she really didn't have a choice. She was stuck with him following her around for the next five days. She sighed. At least Graham would also be with her all week.

She smiled over at the handsome CEO as he dutifully flipped through the airline safety card. *How responsible.* A quality she liked in a man. This was exactly the kind of guy she needed in her life. Maybe she could convince him to stay with her in her suite this week … to protect her, of course.

First, they'd have to get past what happened on Saturday. After the little bout of mistaken identity in the mud room, she'd met Graham at the coffee bar where she'd made sure to stress how she'd thought it was *him* enjoying the treatment, not Jacob.

He'd laughed it off and told her maybe she could introduce him to the mud room another time.

After a long day of finalizing the last details for the expo, Graham had called it an early evening, saying he would grab room service for dinner. She understood. The man had a million things on his mind. He'd given her a warm hug in the resort's parking lot and kissed her forehead. Not quite the day she had envisioned for them.

But then again, she hadn't planned to be caught nearly naked, giving another man a rubdown, either.

She shook off any lingering thoughts of Jacob, concentrating on Graham. Maybe once the expo kicked off, she could help him relax a bit. He did seem somewhat preoccupied this morning—agitated even. He'd been concerned about Jacob's assignment in particular, mentioning more than once that he worried what attendees would think if they saw law enforcement guarding the exhibit. She assured him Jacob wouldn't be in uniform, and they would barely know he was there. That seemed to satisfy Graham.

Their plane took off on time, soaring through the cloudless sky. Thirty minutes later, they'd reached cruising altitude. While she pulled out her National Tea Association magazine to catch up on her industry reading, Graham settled in for a little catnap and was out like a light in no time with his head tilted back and mouth slightly ajar.

Ashley stole a peek at his features. Zoe had it all wrong. He and Jacob looked nothing alike. She glanced over again. Okay, maybe they did a little. Clearly enough for her to mistake the two in the mud bath.

Her gaze slid down his arms. The one thing Graham unfortunately didn't have was Jacob's biceps. She hated to admit it, but the deputy was cut solid. Her hands could have had a field day kneading those muscles. She grimaced.

Ashley, you need to get a grip. Graham is the guy for you. Not Jacob. The suave, suit-wearing tea expert was the one she should be thinking about massaging, not the stupid Emerald Springs reject who had been mean to her since they were kids.

She flipped through her magazine, not really paying attention to anything on the pages. Her thoughts had grabbed onto Jacob's biceps and didn't seem to want to let go.

And if she were completely honest, his arms weren't the only parts on his body that had gotten her attention. The image of his tight butt as he'd gotten out of the tub flashed in her mind, causing her to stir in her seat.

"What's all the squirming about?"

She didn't have to look up to know the owner to that question.

"Going back to join the Mile High Club?" she asked, not taking her eyes off her magazine.

"Already a member."

She looked up. "Why does that not surprise me?"

He pointed to a sleeping Graham. "Doubt you'll get inducted anytime soon."

Ashley flipped her page, not giving him the satisfaction of a response. What a jerk. Some things would never change.

A couple minutes later, Jacob passed her, heading back to his seat. Guess he was just really using the lavatory. Dressed casually, he looked pretty darn cute. She rarely saw him in anything but his deputy uniform, but today he had on loose fitting dark jeans and a white buttoned shirt, his hair gelled up. He almost looked like a guy she'd want to offer to buy her a drink on a Saturday night at Blush.

If she didn't hate him so much.

She watched as a pretty flight attendant flirted with him. Of course. Every woman seemed to fall for his charm. They didn't know him like she did. How cruel he could really be with his sharp insults. He'd rarely had a nice word for her growing up.

She leaned back in her seat. Well, there had been that one night their senior year of high school where Jacob's behavior toward her had been completely out of character.

After scoring the game-winning shot to send the Emerald Springs Cardinals to the state championship, Jacob had marched over in the sea of players, cheerleaders, and fans, picked her up, and asked her to the prom. She'd shot him down in front of the entire school.

"Miss, would you care for anything to drink?"

The flight attendant's question ended Ashley's trip down memory lane. "No, I'm good, thanks."

That night easily went down as one of the worst nights in her high school career. The next day, the halls had been abuzz over what Jacob had done and how Ashley had humiliated him. Worse, the school newspaper had run a picture of her and Jacob in each other's arms when he had hoisted her up. Ashley had torn up her copy and marched into the newspaper's office demanding they retract the photo.

The editor, a mousy nobody, laughed in her face and told her the cheerleaders didn't rule the school and there would be no retraction.

Ashley stared down the plane's aisle, stopping at Jacob's head. What had possessed him to ask her to prom like he did all those years ago? He must have known she was dating one of his teammates … everyone did. Did the all-around athlete simply get caught up in the moment? Perhaps.

A flight attendant's voice filled the plane, announcing they'd started their final decent. Good. This mental trip back to high school had given her a headache. Ashley sat up and rubbed her temples.

She never gave much thought to Jacob's bizarre behavior that night. Since high school, they went about their business, not really getting in each other's way.

That all seemed to change last week. Was karma getting her back for a lifetime of cheap shots? He'd dished out plenty of his own. At basketball games, he would often tell her she had nice legs but would follow up by saying that it was too bad they were on her. She could hear her teenage voice shouting back, "They'll never be around you."

She sighed. After the expo, they could return to their pattern of avoiding each other.

Their plane landed on time, and a few minutes later she and Graham headed for baggage claim, Graham now with his suit jacket draped over his arm. She wondered what it would be like to see him in something more casual. Would he look as cute as Jacob did earlier?

She scanned baggage claim for the deputy but came up empty. He must have decided to take a separate cab to the hotel.

Probably for the better. She really didn't want to put Graham in the awkward position of having to engage in small talk with the guy she mistakenly rubbed down. That would be painful.

After picking up their luggage, they jumped into a cab and headed for the hotel. Graham had a number of meetings with the catering and hotel staff scheduled. Ashley would be accompanying him on a walk-through of the attached convention center later that afternoon.

Until then, she planned on finalizing her presentation for a newcomers workshop that she was asked to run tomorrow morning for all industry professionals attending the Tea Expo for the first time.

"So, I'll meet you at the convention center in an hour for the walk-through." Graham checked his watch.

"Yes." She nodded, taking in the hotel's gorgeous lobby that overlooked San Diego Bay. The attendees were going to love having an ocean view.

They took the elevator up to their floors. Graham was on the fourth, but she was all the way up on the twenty-eighth. Could they be any farther apart? She filed a mental note that any rendezvous had to happen in her suite, because going up twenty floors in the previous day's clothes wasn't going to happen.

The doors opened and Graham stepped out. "See you in a few."

"Sounds good."

"Oh, and Ashley …"

"Yes."

"We're going to have a great week. Maybe we can find a mud bath." He winked.

The doors closed and Ashley smiled, hugging herself in celebration of his suggestion. She and Graham were back on track.

She tapped her fingers on the elevator panel, impatiently waiting to reach her floor. As soon as she got to her room, she'd call to see if the hotel had an in-house spa. A mud bath might be a tall order, but she could definitely see them enjoying side-by-side couple massages.

Reaching her floor, she wheeled her suitcase around the corner, following the sign to her suite. She stopped in her tracks at the site down the hall. "This can't be happening," she muttered as she watched Jacob jam a key into a lock.

He looked over. "Howdy, neighbor."

Sure enough her room was next to his. "We are not staying next to each other."

"Why?" He waggled his eyebrows. "Afraid of the temptation?"

"You wish. This is your doing, isn't it?"

"Hey, don't blame me. Talk to your uncle."

"I will." She paused. "Let's get something straight. Just because you're here all week and staying next door, it doesn't mean we need to interact or hang out or anything. I'm here to work. I've got meetings, a presentation, and an exhibit to run … Thanks to Adam, I have to do it all by myself. I don't need you interfering." She squared her shoulders and stared straight into his eyes. "Is that clear, deputy?"

Jacob leaned down, giving her a nice whiff of his familiar cologne. Why was he always getting into her personal space?

And why did she never seem to have the wherewithal to back away? "Well, is that clear?" she repeated, voice cracking.

"Crystal." He opened his door and left her once again alone to fill up on his scent.

CHAPTER SEVEN

Jacob stood off to the side of the convention center and scanned the large 500,000 square-foot exhibit space. Like it or not, this would be his home for the next four days and starting tomorrow, would fill up with thousands of tea industry professionals, buyers, and connoisseurs alike.

How anyone could get this excited about a drink—a nonalcoholic one no less—he didn't quite understand. Yet, judging by the bustling activity around him, plenty of people were eager to get this shindig on the road.

Jacob hadn't seen Ashley this morning but expected her arrival any minute. As far as he knew, she'd retired early last night. He hadn't heard a sound until her alarm went off at 7:00 a.m. A tray outside her door this morning indicated she'd ordered room service for dinner.

It would make his life easier if she retired early every night while here. Somehow he doubted that was going to happen. How he was going to keep Ashley away from Graham, he still hadn't figured out.

He showered and headed down to the convention center an hour later, meeting with the security director to discuss the plan for the Emerald Tea Farm exhibit. The hotel's security staff had been accommodating and flexible with his demands—no doubt because Richard had called them ahead of time.

Still, he imagined a lot of planning went into exhibitor space and felt badly about the wrench he'd thrown in their lap, which created a lot of scrambling at the last minute.

He raked his hand through his hair and studied the exhibit. The Emerald Tea Farm trademark double tea leaf logo was displayed prominently on a banner hung up by two poles.

Ashley wasn't going to be happy. Adam had said the Whitmans normally had a booth to the left as attendees first walked in. They were accustomed to having the highest foot traffic area in the exhibit hall.

Not this year.

He and the head of security had walked through every inch of the hall and decided that the Whitmans' exhibit would be set up in a less prominent space, up against the west wall and far from any entry points. If someone wanted to mess with Emerald Tea Farm, they would have to cross the entire floor to do it.

Jacob also made sure that a security camera was pointed directly at the booth at all times.

Finally, he'd requested a full list of exhibitors, complete with names and contact information. He would spend the morning grabbing a coffee and poring over the names. Not that he expected to recognize any of the major players in the tea industry. Maybe he could fax the list to Adam and Richard for help with that.

He knew who wasn't on it. Before leaving, he'd talked to his brother-in-law to see if the Prevosts would be exhibiting. Alan's father had decided to skip it this time around, preferring to wait until next year when the expo was in London.

Not that Jacob ever suspected Alan's family of doing anything criminal. While it was true the Whitmans were incredibly wealthy, he suspected their international competitor had way more net worth.

He turned and glanced over at center stage where Graham had been for the last ten minutes practicing his opening remarks. Jacob studied the CEO. Could he be a suspect? The questionable exchange between Ashley's boyfriend and Carlos outside The Rusty Tap still bothered him.

That the CEO of a competitive tea farm appeared to deliberately meet up with one of his sister's hired hands didn't smell right.

Jacob had considered sharing what he saw that night with Richard and Adam, but he wanted more proof. If Graham was behind any or all of the incidents, Jacob doubted he'd do anything at the expo, knowing the Whitmans had sent law enforcement to keep an eye on things. However, maybe Graham would show his hand in other ways.

And if he did, Jacob would be ready.

One thing was for sure, if these acts were sabotage and Graham was involved, Jacob would need to stick close to Ashley and make sure she didn't get mixed up with this dipshit.

He smirked. He had made sure her room was right next to his and far from Graham's.

"What the hell is going on?"

He turned and caught his breath. Ashley stood before him in a sexy, black skirt and matching jacket. Her long hair was pulled back in a tight ponytail. The black wire-rimmed glasses she sported made her look incredibly hot. He'd never seen this look on her.

Maybe he hadn't been paying attention, but what stood in front of him right now caused his heart to race.

"Why is my exhibit over here?" Her hands went to her hips as her eyes narrowed.

The meeting planner who accompanied her was the first to speak. "I'm so sorry, Ms. Whitman. We were just following orders."

"Whose?"

"Mine." Jacob grabbed Ashley's hand. "Let's go talk."

She yanked it away. "We'll talk right here, thank you. Please explain why the Emerald Tea Farm exhibit is against *this* wall where no one will see it."

"I think you're exaggerating just a bit. It's a lovely space." He smiled and that act seemed to tick her off even more.

"I'm calling Adam."

"Go ahead. He's the one who set up the meeting between me and the convention center's security, where we determined that this space right here would be the best for you."

"What do you know about prime exhibit space?" She turned back to the meeting planner. "I'm sorry for the misunderstanding. Please move it to the original space in the exhibit specs. If anyone has a problem with it, they can talk to Graham."

"Ash, it's not going to happen," Jacob said, this time injecting firmness into his tone.

She shook her head. "Enlighten me, deputy. Since you're apparently an expert, why are you insisting it be here?"

"Because you have to cross the entire exhibit floor to get to it; there's no easy access, and …" he pointed to the small security camera mounted from the ceiling, "It's the best angle to catch anything on film in the unlikely event that we need to."

"Exactly. My career is going down the tube for something that is unlikely to happen. I'll be the laughingstock of the tea industry."

"Do you really think this expo is going to make or break you?"

Her scowl indicated he really needed to shut up. "Why don't we go get some coffee? Maybe some tea?" He smiled meekly, cringing inside. What man asked a woman if she wanted to get tea?

She shook her head. "I have a presentation in twenty minutes. I really need to set up."

"You're presenting today?"

"Yes." She pulled up her suit jacket. "You should come. Maybe you'll learn something about a successful farm. Could take some notes for your sister."

"Maybe I will," he said, ignoring her wise crack about Split Acres. He'd rather undergo a root canal without any Novocaine than sit through a presentation about tea trends. He'd keep those feelings to himself.

"Good morning." Graham came up behind Ashley and put his arm around her. "Jacob," he acknowledged coolly.

"Hi, Graham," he replied, trying not to act like he'd like to punch the guy's lights out.

"Nice to see you dressed around Ashley."

"The day's early," Jacob shot back.

Ashley rolled her eyes and patted Graham's hand, still draped around her shoulder. "The exhibits are really looking great."

"They are, aren't they? Why is yours over here?"

She shrugged. "It wasn't my decision."

"Ashley, we've been over this." Jacob's irritation started to creep up the back of his neck; however, this was a great opportunity to watch Graham's reaction. He studied the tea farmer carefully as Ashley explained why her exhibit had moved.

Graham appeared neutral. "Well, this is a good space, too." He smiled down at Ashley. "The best exhibitors are worth the walk."

"I suppose." She smiled back. If they kissed, Jacob was really going to lose it. He hated himself for feeling that way.

"You ready for your session?" Graham continued to stare at the Whitman exhibit space.

"As ready as I'll ever be."

"Good. Let's check in after lunch. I need to go speak to the audiovisual technician. I'm not sure the microphone will project my voice." He headed toward the stage.

"See you," she called out, grinning the entire time.

Jacob laughed.

Her smile turned upside down. "Why are you laughing?"

"I just realized something."

"What?"

"Your subconscious knew it wasn't Graham in the mud bath."

"What are you talking about? Of course I thought it was him."

"Oh, come on. Mr. Uptight?"

"He's not uptight." She paused. "He's reserved."

"Whatever. He probably doesn't even take his shirt off during sex."

"Shut up." She put her palms on him and gave him a little shove. The motion caught him a little off guard, triggering the memory of her sixteen-year-old self doing the exact same thing, although she was wearing a sexy cheerleading outfit then. God, he missed those pompoms.

She turned to leave but spun around, mouth open, and ready to let him have it. No surprise there. The blonde spitfire always had to have the last word—or at least she tried to. Lately, he seemed to be leaving her speechless. He kind of liked this new upper hand he had over her. It probably wouldn't last long.

"Please don't move my exhibit again. I'll be back in a couple of hours to set up."

"I'll be here." He watched as she walked away, his gaze on her hips as they swayed underneath her skirt. That sway and he were old friends. Studying it had been the only way he could give into his feelings and check her out without her knowing.

He turned to look at the space one last time. Now that the location was finalized, he'd wait until Ashley returned and then assist her with set up. What would he do in the meantime? Maybe it would be fun to see professional Ashley in action.

He strolled across the floor, heading toward the registration desk just outside the main entrance. Once there, three pretty meeting planners pounced on him, ready to assist with any need he had. He laughed. If he wasn't working, this expo might actually be a great place to meet chicks.

Who was he kidding? There was only one blonde he wanted to have fun with. He just wasn't quite sure when—or if—he'd ever have the balls to admit it to her again. His first and only attempt years ago had been spontaneous, stupid, and caused him to crash and burn all over his high school gymnasium.

Even though he wasn't that idiot he was all those years ago, he didn't need that kind of humiliation again.

Better he keep his feelings to himself. Once they returned to their lives in Emerald Springs, they'd go back to their pattern of avoidance and trading insults on the occasions they did run into each other.

He got directions to where Ashley was presenting and took the escalators to the upper level meeting rooms. Whipping out his phone, he checked for any messages.

Nothing, which was kind of odd since either Adam or Richard had called him every morning since he agreed to this assignment. He'd check in with them a little later.

Reaching Ashley's packed meeting room, he took an empty seat in the back. She had already begun, launching into a list of new trends for the tea industry.

It really didn't surprise Jacob to see her controlling the room with her poise and confidence. They'd had several classes in high school together where he'd had to listen to her go on and on when it came time for her to present on some dead author's book or world history. Public speaking was her forte.

The lights dimmed and Ashley crossed the room to begin her slide show presentation. His heart raced as his eyes zoned in on her beautiful, long legs. Her skirt sent the same electric charge through him he used to get from her high school cheerleading uniform.

Even though the black skirt had a little more fabric, it showed off one of her best assets as far as he was concerned. He shook his head, thinking back to the night when she informed him her legs would never be around him. That night had sucked for so many reasons …

And he had no desire to relive them, not when grown up Ashley was turning him on from twenty feet away. Maybe this trip was their opportunity to let go of the past.

He lowered his head and stared at the floor, pretty sure hell would freeze over first. The definition of his last name was pond scum in her book. She'd never give him a chance.

Her voice filled his head and he looked up. He didn't know exactly what she was talking about, but the passion she showed with each word totally turned him on. The attendees in the room asked her questions, and she genuinely seemed interested in their learning. He liked this side of her—it was very hot.

His phone buzzed in his palm and he looked down to see Adam's name. About time. He quietly stepped out of the room.

"Hey, Adam." Two attendees chatted in the hallway near him. Not trusting anyone, he walked over to an empty alcove to continue the conversation in private. "Glad to hear from you."

"Hey, Jacob. How are things going?" Adam asked.

"So far, everything is cool. The exhibit will be set up this afternoon in the location that you, Richard, and I agreed would be best, and I've met with the security staff. Great group. Everyone is on heightened alert."

"Good. Good."

Something wasn't right, Jacob could instantly tell by Adam's flat tone. "Everything okay in Emerald Springs?"

There was a long pause before Adam spoke. "There's been another incident."

CHAPTER EIGHT

Ashley stood staring at Jacob, disbelief written all over her face. "What do you mean my dad's at the sheriff's station? What the hell for?"

"We just have a few questions for him." Jacob leaned back on the makeshift tea bar that had been set up by the convention center staff earlier today. He'd been dreading this conversation since Adam had called him with the news.

"Questions? What kind of questions?" She searched her purse and pulled out her phone. "Is he in some sort of trouble? I need to call him."

"Stop. I just checked in with the sheriff about ten minutes ago." He took a deep breath and braced, knowing what he was about to tell her would make her go ballistic. "Your dad's giving a statement. Some guy jumped him last night."

"*What?*" Her worry broke his heart as her eyes began to water.

"It's not as bad as it sounds." That was a total lie, but he didn't want her to have a public meltdown. She had done such a great job this morning with her presentation; he wanted her to ride that high a little longer. She deserved it.

"Jacob, what happened?" Her voice quivered, and she latched onto his shirt. "You need to tell me now."

He grabbed her hand and gently pulled her aside. "First, I need you to lower your voice and promise me you aren't going to totally lose it."

She pulled away. "Tell me what happened," she demanded.

"Your dad's going to be fine. He's just got a black eye."

Her eyes widened. "Someone beat him up? Who?"

"We don't know, but it happened outside the visitor's center."

"My visitor's center?" Her hand flew to her mouth in utter shock. "I don't understand."

"The bastard broke into it last night and from what Adam said, did quite a number. Sam was working late up at the farmhouse and thought he saw a strange car on the premises parked in front of the visitor's center. When he went down to investigate, someone jumped him."

Ashley sprang into action, tapping on her phone. "I'm calling the airlines. I need to get home immediately." She stopped. "Can you take me to the airport?"

He grabbed her hand. "Wait."

"What?"

"Adam asked that you stay put until he has a chance to talk to you. He said there was no reason for you to come back. He, Daniel, and Chad have the whole situation under control."

"Like I'd listen to him." She shook her head, and he could tell she wasn't having it. "I'm supposed to stay here while my dad is injured and the visitor's center is destroyed because my cousins are 'handling it'?"

"Yes." Even Jacob wasn't sure that was the correct answer. If it had been his dad, he'd have been on the first plane back up the coast. Still, Adam had given him specific instructions to keep Ashley in San Diego and promised that he'd call them both later with an update.

Ashley spotted Graham near the entrance and went running over. So much for him not finding out what happened in Emerald Springs. Jacob cursed himself for not asking her to keep it on the down low, even from Graham.

But then she would have asked why, and he wasn't ready to share his suspicions that—in light of what happened last night—might not have any merit.

Jacob watched Ashley deliver the news and Graham give her a hug. He turned, having no desire to see the scumbag comforting her.

Did what happened to Sam and the visitor's center really mean the Seattle's Pure Tea CEO was off the suspect list?

Maybe. Or maybe what had been in that folder that Graham had passed to Carlos was a payoff for the Split Acres' farm custodian to do his dirty work. Jacob reached for his phone. It was time to fill his boss in on what he saw outside The Rusty Tap and see if Sam had gotten a look at his attacker.

His attention turned back to Ashley, who continued to talk with Graham. One thing was for sure. Jacob was getting her away from that dickhead if it was the last thing he did.

She wasn't going to like it, but Ashley just got herself a round-the-clock bodyguard for the rest of the week.

•••

"What do you mean, 'don't be worried'? Of course I'm concerned," Ashley screamed into her phone.

"Ashley, Uncle Sam's fine," Adam said.

That reassuring tone made her want to lunge into the phone and smack him upside the head. This was her dad, and someone had hurt him. "Where is he?"

He's right here at the farmhouse."

"He's working?"

"No, he's resting upstairs in the guest room."

"Put him on, please."

The phone went silent for several long minutes while Ashley tapped her fingers impatiently on the tea bar.

"Hey, dear," her dad finally said. "How is the expo? It's raining here."

"Everything's fine." Now was not the time to catch up on the expo or give a weather report. "How are you?"

"I'm going to be fine. It's just a black eye." He chuckled. "You should see the other guy."

He's laughing. How can he think this is funny? "Did you see Dr. McDonald?"

"I have an appointment later today."

"And Adam or Uncle Richard will drive you, right?"

"Oh, honey. Don't you worry about me."

But she was worried. Someone had deliberately hurt her father, who was by far the most important person in her life. She gulped. What if it was the same man who attacked Daniel? "Have you talked to the police?"

"Yes. I've told them all I know."

"Do you want me to come home?" She looked down at her watch. "Maybe I could catch an afternoon flight."

"No, Ashley. We need you there. Richard and Patty will help if I need anything. Concentrate on the expo and representing Emerald Tea Farm. Can you do that for me?"

She recognized the fact her family wanted her to stay put, although she didn't like it one bit. "Yes, Dad. I love you."

"Love you, too. Here's Adam."

Adam came back on. "We'll check in with you later today, Ash."

"You'll keep an eye on him, right?"

"Of course. Patty's going to swing by his house and bring him dinner tonight."

"I wish he would stay with Uncle Richard," she said.

"I know. We'll ask him again. I know you're worried, but really … other than the shiner, he appears to be okay."

"Well, I guess that's good." She paused. "So how bad is the visitor's center?"

"It's completely destroyed."

"You're kidding." Her breath caught in her chest as she forced out the next question with a low voice. "What did they do?"

"Nothing that can't be restored."

"Adam, tell me. That visitor's center is my baby. Enough sugar coating. What did they do?" she asked, teeth gritted.

"They ransacked the place, smashed the display, overturned the tea bar, sliced all the pictures on the wall, and spray-painted the whole area."

She gasped. "Holy mother of God. Is the sheriff's department involved?"

"Yes, and once they are done gathering evidence, we will begin cleanup and have it up and running as soon as possible."

They talked for a few more minutes before Adam had to take a phone call. The knot in her stomach twisted tighter just thinking about her poor visitor's center and all the work she'd put into it. To say she felt violated was an understatement.

Ashley scanned the exhibit hall, wondering when Jacob would be back. After dropping the bomb about her dad, he'd given her space to talk to her family. Perhaps he was off working on the investigation.

She reached for a box and began to unpack the supplies she'd shipped earlier. With all the chaos, she hadn't had a minute to start setting up her booth. She didn't even want to anymore.

All she wanted to do was hop the next flight up the coast. But since her dad and Adam had vetoed it, it was time to concentrate on the job at hand.

She positioned one blade of her scissors on the closed box and sliced it open. This was all Adam's fault. He should have never pulled him from the trip. If her dad had come with her, he would have never been in harm's way.

Over the next hour, she unpacked her boxes, draped the logo branded skirting over the tables, and plugged in her equipment to make the tea samples. Once she dove in, she found it cathartic, taking her mind off what had happened back home.

She knew deep down that if her dad was seriously injured, they'd have asked her to come home. Still, she planned on checking in on him every few hours, whether he liked it or not. If he even hinted that he was in any sort of pain or his vision was giving him trouble, she was out of there.

Ashley bent down and pushed her empty boxes underneath the tea bar. The Emerald Tea Farm exhibit had really come together. Even if it wasn't going to be in her preferred location, the spot Jacob had insisted on wasn't nearly as bad as she thought it would be. Attendees were in for a special treat.

She stood, brushed off her blouse and skirt, and admired her work. The sample tea bar was stocked and ready to serve; the tea spa facial and mini-massages area set up with comfy chairs; and the interactive exhibit displayed all of the farm's merchandise prominently where attendees could see, touch, and smell all of the tea products she had shipped in.

She wished her family could see it. Maybe she could talk Jacob into making himself useful and filming the exhibit with his phone. Send some photos to Instagram for the company's website. That was a great idea. Filming attendees enjoying the tea samples and mini-spa treatments could provide some fun footage they could later throw up on their website. Perhaps she could ask people who sampled the tea to give short testimonials on what the blends reminded them of.

She reached over, grabbed her notepad, and examined her to-do list. Crossing out items on it always gave her such satisfaction. The only thing she had left to do was open the spa test products for the complimentary facials. She reached into the last box on the tea bar, pulling out the green tea sugar facial scrub.

Opening the lid, she poked her finger in the grainy mixture and rubbed it into the top of her hand. For some reason, it wasn't rubbing in easily but clumping in a small ball. This wouldn't work. Maybe she could dilute the mixture? But would that make it too thin? She needed someone to test out the scrub before her volunteers started exfoliating attendees.

"Hey, can I help?" Jacob sauntered up to the booth.

"I was wondering when you might return."

"Miss me?"

"Hardly."

"How's Sam doing?"

She sighed. "He swears he's fine. Do you have any news on who might have done this?"

"No. Not yet. Some deputies are returning to the farm this afternoon."

"Oh."

"Say, your exhibit looks great. You've been busy this afternoon."

"Yes, I have." She shrugged.

"Anything I can do to help?" Jacob asked again.

"No." She glanced down at the facial sugar grains in her hand—no, that was a silly idea. But the deputy's face was perfect for scrubbing. And this man owed her for tagging along like a babysitter. "I could use some assistance."

"Sure. What do you need?"

"Come sit." She motioned for him to take a seat in one of the spa chairs.

He obediently took a seat. "What now? You're not going to slather me in mud again, are you? I'm kind of overdressed."

"Very funny." She held the facial scrub container in her palm. "So, one of the things we're doing starting tomorrow is giving complimentary mini-facials with our green tea sugar scrub. Since you're so fond of exfoliation, I thought maybe you could be my sample model."

He leaned back. "You know, I recall you seemed to enjoy our time together in the mud bath just as much as I did."

"Let's not forget I thought you were another man."

"If that's your story." He smirked and settled back in the chair, closing his eyes.

She scooped some of the scrub into her hand and began to massage Jacob's face, spreading the grainy mixture all over. She couldn't help but soak up his features, from the cute dusting of freckles on his nose to his dark, sexy lashes and incredibly full, kissable mouth.

She swiped some scrub across his lips, and that simple act caused her hand to tingle. Pulling it away, she gave it a shake, wishing away any sensual residue from his touch. "Now don't move and don't speak unless you want a glob of green tea sugar scrub in your mouth."

He raised his hand and gave her a thumbs-up sign.

She reached for a white hand towel she'd unpacked earlier. "Okay, stay still for five minutes. I'll be right back. I just want to wet a towel to help remove the scrub."

Heading into the bathroom gave her a few minutes alone to digest what Jacob had said about the mud bath. He'd admitted he'd enjoyed it. That was news to her.

"Stop it, Ashley," she ordered her reflection in the mirror. "You are not going there with Jacob Sanders of all people. You hate him. He hates you. Period."

She turned on the faucet and saturated the towel with cold water. If she hated him, why did his touch make her tingle, not to mention she couldn't get enough of his scent every time he was around?

Squaring her shoulders, she returned to the exhibit room. *Graham is the guy for you.*

Ashley noticed that two pretty meeting planners had joined Jacob and were touching his face, giggling all the while.

God, she couldn't even leave him for a second without women swarming in.

"It doesn't matter," she muttered, joining the trio.

"What doesn't matter?" Jacob asked.

"Nothing." She unfolded the towel.

"Can you take this off now?"

"Yes," she said flatly and began wiping his face.

"Thanks for keeping me company, ladies. I'll see you around."

Ashley could have sworn he'd made both the meeting planners blush before they scurried away. They were probably in competition to see which one would be invited up to his suite. She wrinkled her nose and pressed down around his nose.

He hands reached up and grabbed the towel. "Ashley, what the hell. Are you trying to suffocate me?"

"Why would I do that?" She blinked innocently. "Thanks for your help. I think the scrub is fine for tomorrow."

"Glad I could be of assistance. Catie and Emma are going to buy some of that scrub when you open."

"Catie and Emma," she repeated. "Do they know that you don't come with it?"

He raised an eyebrow. "Something the matter?"

"No." She busied herself at the tea bar while he checked his phone messages a few yards away. Some afternoon tea was in order. She scanned the room. It was strange that Graham hadn't stopped by all afternoon.

Jacob returned and shoved his phone in his pocket.

"Any news on my dad's assailant?"

"I can't really talk about it."

"So there is news."

He shook his head. "Not really. Can I get you anything?"

She handed him a thermos. "Could you fill this with water? I want to brew some tea."

"Sure. Be right back." He hurried off. While he was gone, Ashley took a few minutes to greet her neighboring exhibitors and learn more about their products. For all she knew about tea, there was so much more to learn. Jacob returned with Catie by his side, carrying a tray of large cookies. Looks like she'd won the battle for the deputy's attention. Ashley shook her head. If they only knew the Jacob she did.

Although, he'd been pretty awesome today. Maybe she didn't know him as well as she thought. Maybe he'd changed.

"Thanks, Catie, for the snack. You're a doll." He set the thermos down and took the plate from his companion's hand. The meeting planner headed back out of the exhibit, but not before turning around and giving Jacob a flirtatious smile.

"Looks like you have a fan."

"I have many fans." He winked. "All over the country."

She searched for her tea cups in the box on the bar. "And South Africa, too," she said, not thinking what she was saying.

"South Africa?" He raised an eyebrow.

Crap. There was no way she was going to admit she had spied on him and Kimi in the airport and witnessed their goodbye kiss. "And Europe and Asia … I'm sure your fan base is global." She laughed nervously, trying to recover from her blunder.

He pulled up a barstool and took a seat. "I'd settle for one in Emerald Springs."

The cups rattled in her hands. Who was he talking about? She set one down in front of him. "Well, I do remember Carly Patterson had quite the crush on you."

"Wait. How did I not know this?"

"Oh, please. I know she propositioned you to get out of a speeding ticket just last year."

He chuckled. "You knew about that?"

"Girls share everything." She shrugged.

"Well, I didn't take her up on that offer. I hope she shared that."

Her friend had conveniently left that part out. Relief rushed through Ashley.

"Well, all the girls thought you blossomed senior year."

He leaned forward, placed his elbow on the bar, and rested his chin in his palm. "All the girls?"

If she didn't know exactly what he was implying with that question, her warm cheeks certainly did. "High school was a long time ago."

"I couldn't agree more." He straightened and pointed to the carafe he'd fetched for her. "So what are we making? Herbal, green, or black?"

She sighed. "Do you know anything about tea?"

"Sure. It's hot … and good for you … and earthy, crunchy people drink it. How am I doing?"

"Not so well." She reached in her basket for a Cherry Berry Spice packet, her favorite. "Let me show you what this wondrous leaf can really do for you." She poured the water into the cup and then took the tea packet and gently broke the water's surface. The tiny bubbles forming made her smile.

She motioned for him to peer in. "See those bubbles."

"Yeah?"

"That means kisses are coming."

She looked straight into his chocolate eyes, not expecting their warm response. It took all of her strength not to reach over, grab his head, and kiss those lips.

He nodded down to the cup, not breaking eye contact. "Does it indicate whose lips those might be?"

Ashley's heart began to race. Why was this man of all the men on this planet having this effect on her?

She took a deep breath. "Um … maybe it will be …" Out of the corner of her eye, she saw someone barreling over to them. She reluctantly looked away from Jacob and her mouth dropped. "Mom?"

"You want me to kiss my mom?"

"No, my mom … is here." Ashley stood in horror as her mother made her way to them.

Dressed in a tight, black mini-dress and large, gold, hoop earrings, Elizabeth Whitman sauntered through the exhibit hall like she owned it, turning heads of the male exhibitors and convention staff.

"Darling! How is my beautiful girl?" She threw her arms around Ashley.

Ashley returned the embrace with a short hug. "Mom, what are you doing here?"

"Why, I've come to see you. You said you were going to be here in your e-mail." She paused and her mouth flew open. "Oh … my … God. Jacob Sanders, is that you?"

"Yes, ma'am. It's nice to see you, Mrs. Whitman."

"What on earth are you doing here? Is Joe finally in the tea business?"

He chuckled. "No ma'am." His eyes met Ashley's.

"He's on assignment," Ashley interrupted.

Her mom squeezed Jacob's arm. "My you've grown up." She winked. "And filled out."

Ashley bit her lip. Leave it to her mom to start flirting with Jacob. This reunion so was not happening here. "Mom, I'm really busy right now. Could we catch up later?"

"Would you like to have dinner?" Her mother turned to Jacob, not waiting for Ashley to answer. "I hope you will join us." Her mother's hand appeared to have made its way to his back within an inch of his ass.

"Would love to."

Ashley stood, trying to process what was happening while her mother continued to flirt brazenly with Jacob.

She hadn't thought this day could get any worse, but it just did.

CHAPTER NINE

Think, Ashley, think. She paced in her suite. She had no desire to take her mom up on her invitation to have dinner with her tonight, but she also knew her mother would unlikely take no for an answer.

It wasn't that she didn't want to spend time with her mom in theory, but the expo was not the place for a mother-daughter reunion. Too much was riding on it, and she couldn't trust that her mother wouldn't ruin everything.

This afternoon's strut through the hall in her tight outfit was tame to what Ashley knew her mom was capable of. Get her around a crowd, there was no telling what she might do or whom she'd hit on. Ashley didn't need that kind of embarrassment.

The only saving grace was that her dad wasn't there. Now that would have been a disaster of epic proportions. A black eye he seemed to be dealing with just fine, but her mother? A completely different kind of pain.

Jacob had followed her to her suite and now sat relaxed on the sofa, drinking a beer he'd raided from her minibar.

She stopped pacing and stared at Jacob, unable to tell if he empathized with her or found the whole situation utterly amusing. Probably the latter.

And why not? Everyone in Emerald Springs knew her parents' embarrassing back story. Her mom had never been happy with her dad's decision to work for Uncle Richard, wanting him to set his sights higher and run his own company. Her father tried to make her happy, building her a four-bedroom, two-bath dream house looking out over Lake Emerald and purchasing the Coffee Queen, which he touted would be bigger than Starbucks if they played their cards right.

Mom had pretty much laughed in his face over that purchase and then took up with a much younger man she'd met on a weekend girls' getaway to Palm Springs. Shortly after, her parents separated, leaving Ashley heartbroken for her dad and pissed off at her mother.

Sure, it annoyed Ashley that on occasion her dad took far too much credit than he should for her ideas, but she knew how proud he was of her. That was more than she could say of her mother. Ashley plopped down next to Jacob and pointed to his beer can. "You know, I have to pay for that."

"I think your family can afford it."

He put his arm over the sofa; his hand brushed her shoulder for a moment before he moved it up. Her spine shivered and she quickly straightened.

"So, how long has it been since you've seen her?" he asked.

"My college graduation."

"Really? That long."

"Yeah, I mean we e-mail and talk on the phone every once in a while."

"It must be hard."

"She wouldn't be so bad if she wasn't such a ..." She clenched her hands.

"Gold digger?"

"Pretty obvious, huh?"

"Not really. I just know the backstory from my mom." He smiled. "Remember the time she and my mom took you, Colleen, and me to the Seattle Zoo and they made you and me hold hands the whole entire time?"

Ashley studied Jacob. *What an odd thing for him to remember.* True, though. She glanced down, recalling how safe she felt that day while they looked at the tigers and bears. Could his hand still offer that protection?

Jacob jumped off the sofa. "Why don't we take her up on her offer and have dinner? I know for a fact you've been surviving on coffee, and probably tea, the last twenty-four hours. It would do us both some good to get out of this hotel and mix up the scenery."

Her eyebrow went up at his suggestion. "You really want to have dinner with my mother?"

"Two blondes on my arm? Hell yeah."

She couldn't help but laugh. "Better not say that around Mom. You might be her next conquest."

"Don't want a young stepdad?" he asked jokingly.

"Not even funny." She sighed. It would be nice to get out of the hotel and see a little of San Diego. Having Jacob with her would ensure conversation was light and didn't dive into areas Ashley didn't want it to. Besides, he was right, she hadn't eaten much today and was ready to gnaw off her hand.

"Fine. I'll let my mother know." She reached for her cell phone. "I should probably invite Graham, too."

Jacob threw his hands up in the air. "There goes the evening."

"Stop it. He's really not that bad."

"That's an interesting choice of words."

"What?" Ashley picked up the receiver.

"'He's really not that bad.'"

"He isn't. What's your point?"

By the glint in his eye, she knew he was going to say something that would either piss her off or entice her to tear off his clothes. She was starting to wonder if, when it came to Jacob, hate and lust were one and the same.

"If I were your boyfriend, you'd never say that."

She set the phone down. This flirting had to stop. Right here, right now. Sure, they called a truce this afternoon and had some fun playing with the spa products and then the whole tea bubbles and kisses thing, but this was Jacob Sanders. *Her nemesis.*

This flirty, suggestive banter wasn't their norm, and right now she couldn't handle the universe messing with her any more today than it already had. She hurried to the door and flung it open. "Pick me up at 6:00 p.m., deputy."

Jacob obliged, but not before reaching up and giving her ponytail a soft tug. "It's a date."

CHAPTER TEN

Jacob hopped in the shower, letting the hot water run across his face. What a long ass day. Not his usual routine of paperwork in the morning, cruising in his squad car in the afternoon. Spending the day with a bunch of tea enthusiasts was a bit draining to say the least.

But he wouldn't trade this afternoon with Ashley for all the tea in China.

True to his word, he'd stuck to her like glue and that invisible adhesive between them wasn't going to fall off anytime soon.

That her eccentric, screwball mother showed up was a godsend as far as he was concerned. He hoped Elizabeth planned on staying for the whole expo. It would make Jacob's life easier if he didn't have to pry Ashley away from Graham to keep an eye on her.

He jumped out of the shower and wrapped a towel around his waist, leaning for a second on the bathroom cabinet. Elizabeth's visit could also potentially keep Ashley entertained in the evenings. Another reason he'd been happy to see the ex-Mrs. Whitman.

Flirting with Ashley this afternoon was an unexpected surprise. Her giving him an impromptu facial like she did had been awesome. That light massage had given him quite a jolt, and it wasn't from the green tea or whatever the hell she'd put on his face.

And the whole bubbles thing in the tea predicting kisses. *Please.* It was the mud bath all over again. She wanted to kiss him as much as he wanted her to. He just needed a little more one-on-one time to make it happen.

He grabbed a second towel to dry off his face. Why was he even thinking this way again? For so many years he'd buried his feelings for the pretty Whitman. Did he really want to reveal them now?

And what if he was wrong and his Sanders name really did still repulse her?

Moving to the bedroom, he grabbed his wallet and searched for the one piece of evidence that would inevitably expose how he really felt. His fingers touched the crumbled newspaper as he unfolded it and smiled down at the picture of a seventeen year-old image of himself with a teenage Ashley in his arms. The newspaper photo taken after he'd made that record-breaking shot had been in his desk at home for years, but last week he moved it to a new residence in his wallet.

Could he ever tell her the truth about that night—that he was trying to shield her from seeing her boyfriend kiss her best friend? That had been his real motivation for spinning her around in his arms and away from the scene that would break her heart.

Then he'd got caught up in the moment and asked her to prom. That question had even surprised him.

He grabbed his toothbrush, pumped some toothpaste, and brushed. Was it even worth bringing up something that happened so long ago? Maybe if he did, she'd understand he wasn't always the jerk she thought he was and that he'd been looking out for her that night.

He quickly dressed, realizing he needed to be at Ashley's door in five minutes, and threw on a blazer. Why not show Ashley he could clean up and look every bit as businesslike as Graham? Not that he really wanted to be compared to that ass clown. God, he hoped Graham wouldn't be joining them for dinner.

Stepping outside his room, he folded the newspaper clipping, slid it back in his wallet, and knocked on Ashley's door.

"Perfect timing. Can you zip me up?" Ashley turned and lifted her hair, revealing her beautifully tanned back.

"Um … sure." Jacob took a deep breath and his hand clumsily tried to pull up the zipper to her sleeveless, black dress. Preoccupied by her floral perfume that drifted down deep into his lungs, his hand stopped halfway up.

"Is it stuck?" she asked.

He gave the zipper a final yank. "All set. Anything else I can do to you … er … I mean for you?" *Smooth, dumbass. Real smooth.*

She scrambled across the living room and slid her feet into a pair of black stilettos, completely oblivious to his blunder. "Okay, I talked to Graham. He's going to order room service and do some work this evening, so it's just you, me, and my mother."

Yes! "Sorry to hear that." He offered his arm. "Shall we?"

She blew past him, ignoring his offer. Apparently their casual flirting from this afternoon was over.

"You know, you could try to enjoy this evening." He caught up to her as they headed for the elevator, stuffing his hands into his pant pockets. "Maybe unwind a bit."

She pushed the elevator button and raked her hand through her curls. Jacob couldn't help but wonder what it would be like for his hands to dive into her soft waves. He bet if he did it once, he'd never want to stop.

He let out a small groan.

"Everything okay?"

"Yeah, yeah. I hate waiting for the elevator." *Next to a beautiful woman who I'd rather take back to my suite and show how much I've wanted her.*

"You're right about me being wound up. I'm sorry. It's just my mother brings out the bitchy side in me."

"Just your mother?" he asked, then instantly regretted it.

Her eyes narrowed. "What's that supposed to mean?"

"Nothing." He entered the elevator.

"Are you implying I'm often in a bad mood?"

"No. Not at all." He grinned and watched the elevator numbers go down. "Just feisty. When being arrested or caught massaging the wrong man."

She rolled her eyes. "That massage was an honest mistake."

He tilted his head back and laughed. "Yep, because your boyfriend and I look so much alike."

"You do!" She paused. "From the back, I mean … covered in mud."

Jacob smirked, loving the pink he brought out in her cheeks—it matched her pretty, pink lipstick. "So Graham's staying in for the night?"

"Yes." The elevator doors opened and she stepped out. "He's got his big keynote luncheon tomorrow, so he wants to write his remarks and get a good night's sl—"

Her sentence stalled and Jacob followed her line of sight to see what had caused it. Straight ahead Graham sat at the bar, appearing engrossed in a beautiful brunette in a tight, blue dress, his hand caressing her knee as she laughed at something he'd said.

"Maybe he's practicing his remarks," Jacob said coolly.

Ashley started to head over, but he grabbed her arm. "Do you really want to do this? Is he worth it?"

"Jacob, let me go." She freed herself from his grasp and took a few steps in Graham's direction. The next few minutes were probably not going to be pretty. Whatever happened, one thing was for sure. He'd be there to pick up the pieces.

He cracked his knuckles. *And kick Graham's ass if he needed to.*

How was it that ten years later, he was once again in the middle of Ashley and another cheating boyfriend? And why was she so attracted to chumps like Graham? She should be with someone who would love her and cherish her and make her feel like the most amazing woman she was.

Ashley suddenly stopped in her tracks. Flinging around, she flew past him. "Let's go."

Jacob quickly followed and once outside, requested a taxi from the concierge. The Mexican restaurant where Elizabeth suggested they meet her was a short ten minutes away.

An agonizing ten minutes. Once in the cab, Ashley's silent brooding took up the entire backseat, suffocating him. He loosened his collar and cracked the window.

"I'm sorry," he finally said, not really knowing what he was apologizing for, but it seemed like the gentlemanly thing to do.

"For what?" She turned from the window; her watery eyes appeared to be doing their best to hold back tears.

"What you saw back there."

She slid her fingers underneath her eyes, catching her tears. "It's not a big deal."

"I think your boyfriend feeling up another woman might qualify as a big deal."

"He's not my boyfriend," she said flatly.

What? Did he hear her right? "I thought you said he was."

"When?"

"Last week. At Emerald Eats. You told me he was your boyfriend."

"We were never a couple." She turned her head back to the window. "I'd rather not talk about it."

Jacob sat completely dumbfounded. *So Ashley had lied about Graham being her boyfriend.* Why had she done that? A deep sense of relief washed over him, realizing that she and the prick weren't as close as she'd led Jacob to believe. It just made his job keeping watch over her a hell of a lot easier.

It was easier on his heart, too.

They arrived at the restaurant, and Jacob paid the taxi driver, hopped out, and walked over to the other side, opening the door.

"Thank you." She took his hand and got out, but just when he thought she'd release it, something unexpected happened. Her fingers threaded through his.

They were standing together on the sidewalk, holding hands like they did years ago at the zoo when they were eight.

He suspected the cougar waiting for them inside might have something to do with this sudden need for protection. He smiled down. "It's only dinner."

"I know." She sighed.

Jacob gave her hand an assuring squeeze. "I'm right here, and afterward if you need to talk about what you saw back at the hotel, I can do that, too." His sincere offer surprised even him, but he meant every word. "We can also call your dad together and check in on him."

"Thank you." She still held onto his hand, making no movement to go into the restaurant. "Today's been kind of …"

"Fucked up?"

That got a sarcastic laugh. "Something like that."

He reached for the entrance door and opened it for her. The colorful restaurant was crowded, but looked inviting and comfortable with a lively mariachi band playing in the corner. Not a usual place he'd spend an evening, but with Ashley next to him—needing him like he knew she did—there was no place he'd rather be.

They spotted her mother at the bar, hands draped all over a bartender. Apparently Elizabeth and Graham had something in common with their public displays of affection.

In a tight, leopard tank top and black leather pants, she'd come to prowl. Jacob laughed to himself, remembering a past New Year's Eve when he was a kid watching the former Mrs. Whitman flirt unabashedly with his dad. Some things never changed.

She caught sight of them and brightened. "Hello, you two!" Her long arms went out to hug Ashley and then Jacob. His hug lasted twice as long as the one she'd given her daughter and just like this afternoon, her hands made their way to his butt.

"You've grown up, Jacob Sanders." She gave his arm a squeeze. "Oh, my. And filled out in all the right places, I see." Even with his blazer as a barrier, his arm felt violated.

"Hi, Mom." Ashley shot her mother a look of disapproval that Jacob easily caught. He moved away from Elizabeth, pulling out a chair for Ashley.

"It's nice to see you, again, Mrs. ..." He realized he didn't know what her married name was these days.

"You were right this afternoon. It's still Whitman."

"Of course it is," Ashley said. "You always liked the name."

Jacob caught the coolness in her voice. This might be a long night if mother and daughter started going at it.

"How's Stuart?" Ashley took her seat and picked up a drink menu. From what Jacob could tell, her first priority was to get alcohol in her as soon as humanly possible. After the day she had, he didn't blame her.

"Oh, darling. Didn't I tell you?" Elizabeth motioned for the waiter. "They make the best sangria here ... anyway, Stuart and I are done."

"Really?" Ashley cocked an eyebrow. "That didn't last long."

"After two years, he became such a bore. Married to his work. Not to mention his selfish kids were always meddling. Honestly, I think I need to set my sights on a younger man." She flashed a smile in Jacob's direction. "With a hot body who, no doubt, knows how to use it."

Jacob leaned back, trying to play dumb after Elizabeth's blatant come-on. Maybe he should be the one holding Ashley's hand for protection.

The ladies ordered a pitcher of sangria while he elected to try one of the restaurant's special Mexican beers. Fruity drinks had never been his thing. They spent the first half hour engaged in idle chitchat. He wasn't sure if it had anything to do with the way Ashley guzzled down her drink and then quickly refilled her glass, but the conversation seemed to be going fine. Mother and daughter caught each up other on their lives, and Ashley even laughed a bit. It was good to see her relax, a side he rarely saw.

Aside from the trip to the zoo and seeing Elizabeth at the Whitman farmhouse for social gatherings before the family feud, he didn't really remember her growing up. However, he could tell after only a few minutes that Ashley was nothing like her mother. Where Ashley had grown up to be a professional powerhouse with both brains and beauty, her mother seemed to lack any type of real sophistication.

"So how are things in Emerald Springs?" Elizabeth asked, swirling a chip in the guacamole dip and taking a bite. "I hear Whitman businesses have been under attack these last few months."

"Who did you hear that from?" Ashley motioned for the bartender to refill their pitcher.

Elizabeth shrugged. "People talk."

"In Emerald Springs, they sure do." Jacob chuckled. "It's under investigation." He paused, "We have a couple of strong leads." *One even here in San Diego currently sucking face with some brunette at the hotel.*

Ashley turned to him and her brow furrowed. "You do? Who?"

"I can't really say."

"I hope you catch the bastard after what he did to Dad."

Elizabeth's eyes widened. "What happened to your father?"

"He's fine." Ashley waved her hand. "He was jumped last night by some hoodlum who vandalized the visitor center."

"Oh." Elizabeth paused for a second. "I'm sorry to hear that. Well, I'm glad he's okay."

"Are you, Mom?"

"Darling, of course. Just because we're not married doesn't mean I'm not concerned about his well-being." She scooted closer to Jacob. "It really doesn't surprise me that he got his ass kicked. Sam was never good with his fists. I bet you, deputy, could hold your own in a fight."

Jacob laughed uncomfortably and sipped his beer.

Elizabeth waved her glass in the air. "I think Marlon Miller is the one behind it. That no good bum. The way he treated Zoe all of these years, pretty much leaving her to fend for herself. Besides, he knows that farm like the back of his hand."

Marlon had definitely been on the top of the short list of suspects, especially after instigating a bar fight at Emerald Eats, but he didn't really have a motive. The town drunk. Yes. But an arsonist, among other things? Jacob wasn't quite sure.

Plus, there's no way Marlon could have jumped Sam and given him that shiner.

"I don't think it's Marlon," Ashley piped in, grabbing the fresh pitcher of sangria and refilling her glass. "He's really trying to clean up his act, and Zoe mentioned that he attended his first Alcoholics Anonymous meeting last week. She believes in him. Time will tell."

"What about Colleen's new husband?" Elizabeth leaned closer to Jacob, touching his arm. "What's he like?"

"He's cool. Really smart and ready to turn things around for Split Acres."

"But isn't he a competitor for Emerald Tea Farm? There could be motive there."

Jacob was impressed by Elizabeth's knowledge. She clearly kept her finger on the gossip even from more than a thousand miles away.

"Nah, it's definitely not the Prevosts. Those guys have way more money than the Whitmans."

"Hmm … Looks like you have a mystery on your hands." She leaned over and stroked Jacob's arm. The mix of her heavy floral perfume and the sangria on her breath churned his stomach.

He smiled, not quite sure how to move his arm away, when all of a sudden he felt a hand on his shoulder.

"Oh, Mom. Stop teasing Jacob." Ashley's finger made tiny circles around the area of his neck that drove him crazy. "He doesn't want to talk about work."

That was an understatement.

The heat she'd generated around his neck caused him to lose his words. "No ... er ... we should probably not do it." He shook his head. "Talk about it ... the case ... I mean. It's ongoing."

Jacob didn't know when his evening had turned, but all through dinner, mother and daughter appeared to be in competition and he was the grand prize. When one grazed his hand, the other ran her hands down his back.

Ashley seemed to be in it to win it. While he studied the desert menu, she ran her hand over his groin, and whispered in his ear loudly enough for her mother to get her intent, "I've always wondered what's underneath your uniform. Care to show me later?"

And that did it. She'd won. His hand flew up for the check because he, Ashley, and his erection were calling it a night.

• • •

Ashley searched inside her clutch for her room key, feeling Jacob's hard body hovering behind her. It was after 11 p.m., and they were alone in the hallway.

"Ash, we need to talk," he said softly.

"About?" She asked the question but didn't have the guts to turn around and face him for the answer.

"What happened in the restaurant?" His hand played in her curls, causing her to lose track of the conversation. She turned, trying to get control of the situation.

"Look, I'm really sorry about that, Jacob. I thought you might need rescuing from my mother." She gazed into his gorgeous, brown eyes, knowing the next sentence cued up to launch from her lips was a lie.

"I was just pretending." *Yep, a big fat one.*

He continued to play with her hair, wrapping a long curl around his finger. "So you stroking me underneath the table and the invitation for later was just for show?"

She pushed his hand away. "Yes, and I'm sorry." She paused, trying to think of a plausible excuse for groping him like she'd done. "You looked out for me all day; I was just returning the favor. Now we're even."

His lips turned up, indicating he wasn't buying it.

She attempted to open her door, jamming the flat, plastic keycard in the slot. It wouldn't unlock. "Dammit."

How did this day get so out of control? Her father being jumped, the visitor's center being destroyed, her mother showing up, Graham feeling up some random tramp … It was like her universe had spun completely out of control. The only truth she knew right now was that the one man who hated her had been there for her through it all.

The man she'd wanted to kiss since she saw him in the airport with Kimi and obviously couldn't handle seeing her mom run her hands all over. She took a deep breath, knowing exactly what she wanted.

She spun around and grabbed onto his blazer. "I want to forget about today. Jacob, can you make me forget?" Not waiting for an answer, she pulled him close and took possession of his lips.

He deepened the kiss, running his hands down her dress and then pulling her in. "I think I can."

Ashley wrapped her arms around his neck and allowed her tongue to glide with his. His body felt warm and secure. Everything was happening so fast, but one thing was clear: she was going to have the deputy in her bed tonight and get from him exactly what she needed.

They stumbled into the suite, and she reached for the light. He immediately pulled her hand down to stop her as they began tearing each other's clothes off. It didn't take long for her to strip him out of his blazer and white collar shirt. His exposed chest left her breathless.

Slowly, her mouth went to work on his neck, kissing him in the spot she knew drove him crazy, the same area she'd kneaded in the mud bath and played with at dinner. Within seconds, he moaned his approval and unzipped her dress, gently removing it off of her shoulders.

She stepped out of it, kicking off her stilettos. How incredible was this one-night stand going to be? Unlike with Graham, with Jacob she knew exactly where they stood. In the morning, they'd go back to despising each other and trading insults.

She brought him over to her bed and ran her hands up and down his bare, muscular arms.

"I drive you crazy, right?"

His lips caressed her ear as he muttered, "Fucking crazy."

She pulled back, blocking him by putting her hand on his chest. "But in a bad way, yes?"

Jacob's eyes were hazy. "Ashley Whitman, you have driven me crazy all of my life."

That's all she needed to hear. She would use him to get through this night, knowing he was doing the same. Nothing would change and no one would ever know.

She unloosened his belt buckle while his hands unhooked her bra strap. They flung the items simultaneously to the floor. Jacob kicked off his shoes while she unzipped his khakis.

He'd rocked those pants with his blazer tonight. A far departure from his deputy outfit. What was underneath it was even better. Her hands splayed over his chest before she pushed him onto the bed.

Jacob never took his eyes off of her as she climbed on top of him. While his fingers tangled in his hair, she nipped at his earlobe and inhaled his delicious scent.

This was really happening. The man who'd pressed her buttons for most of her life was going to give her body an entirely new sensation.

With one swift move, Jacob scooped her up and flipped her onto her back, his eyes penetrating hers for a few seconds before he started a trail of soft kisses down her neck.

He gently massaged her breasts before taking one into his mouth.

"Should we really be doing this?" she murmured.

He glanced up, lightly circling her other breast with his palm. "Do you want me to stop?"

"No," she whispered and arched her back. "God, no."

His lips worked their way back up her body, first kissing the base of her neck before he took full possession of her mouth again. His hard length pressed against her.

"Jacob, I want you." She couldn't help but bring her lips again to the weak spot on his neck, eager to see just how crazy she could drive him. He moaned and rolled to the side.

Had he changed his mind?

He bent down and reached for his khakis, pulled out his wallet, and turned back with the small foil.

Of course, he wasn't leaving. Not when they were just getting started.

He covered his length, and then moved his hands up her body, his lips reuniting with hers.

Breaking the kiss, she searched his eyes. "What were you saying about being crazy about m—"

His lips brushed hers, cutting her off. "You want to have this conversation now?"

She reached down and stroked him with much more urgency than she'd done at the restaurant. "No. Not really."

Cupping her face in his hands, he grinned. "Ms. Whitman. You have the right to remain silent now and enjoy the moment."

She grinned back. "Nothing I do or say will be held against me tomorrow?"

"You have my word."

As he slipped off her panties, she was pretty sure she wasn't going to be quiet. Her nails clenched his back as he entered her. She tilted her head back, enjoying the rhythm they easily found.

He swore, which she knew was an acknowledgment of his own pleasure. Grabbing her hands, he laced them with his over the top of her head.

Her breath quickened as Jacob drove into her, giving her exactly what she'd needed. If this was what it was like to be intimate with a man she hated, she could go on hating Jacob Sanders for all eternity.

• • •

Jacob awoke to Ashley running her hands up and down his back. Someone was feeling frisky again. He smiled and turned to face her. "I thought this was a one-and-done type of thing."

"Well …" She flipped onto her side, flinging her hair over and exposing her neck. "If that's all you want it to be."

"Hell, no." His lips caressed her neck, her soft skin causing him to immediately go hard. "There's another condom in my wallet." He started to roll off the bed, but she threw up her hand.

"I got it." He watched her get out of the bed, her naked body bending down for his wallet, which he'd cast aside after retrieving the first condom earlier.

How had he gotten so lucky? If anyone would have told him he'd be in Ashley Whitman's bed having—without question—the best sex of his life, he would have laughed in their face. Although secretly hoping they were right.

Maybe she was using him to get even with Graham. But the way she'd showered him with kisses and called out his name over and over didn't feel like a rebound. Not to mention her eagerness to get him properly suited up for round two.

"Jacob?"

"Yes, baby." *What was wrong?* She didn't say anything but stood with her back to him. Maybe it was too early to call her by a term of endearment. "Ashley?"

She darted into the bathroom and came out seconds later in a white bathrobe. He knew he was screwed by what she held in her hand.

"Why are you carrying this around?" She flung the newspaper clipping at him and folded her arms.

He sat up and raked his fingers through his hair. The condom in his wallet wasn't going to be used anytime soon.

"Ash …" He set the picture on the night stand, face down. "Why don't you come back to bed, and we'll talk about it."

"How long, Jacob?" She ignored his invitation, eyes narrowed.

"How long what?"

"How long has that picture been in your wallet?"

"Why does it matter?"

"Because this changes everything. This," she pointed to the bed, "was supposed to be a meaningless one-night stand, and now you've gone and ruined it."

He smiled. Her flare for drama didn't really surprise him. No, he'd grown up experiencing it on more than one occasion. What shocked him more was how at ease he felt about her finally knowing the truth.

Well, at least part of it. He didn't plan on taking a trip back to that gymnasium anytime soon.

"You have nothing to say?" She threw her hands up in the air.

"Right now, all you need to know is last night was not meaningless for me."

She sat down on the edge of the bed, head down. "But you hate me, and I hate you."

He sat up and leaned over. "I don't hate you." Touching her face, he tilted her head toward him. "Look at me. Just because it meant something to me, doesn't mean it's ruined. But if you can't handle it, we can go back to the way things were … if that's what you want." He paused. "Is that what you want?"

"That's what I want." She stood, tying her bathrobe tightly around her middle. "You should leave." Storming into the bathroom, the door slammed behind her.

Minutes later, the shower came on. He rolled off the bed and went to the window, looking out at the sun beginning to rise over the quiet bay. Stretching his arms behind his back, he thought about his next move. Going back to his room was probably the best option right now. Let her get ready in private. Today kicked off the expo, and she'd be in full force soon enough.

He had no plans, however, to throw in the towel when it came to exploring this chemistry they had. She could convince herself otherwise, but he knew she'd enjoyed every single minute of their time entangled as much as he did.

So what if she knew his feelings ran deeper. It was high time he was honest with her—and himself for that matter.

As he turned to gather his clothes, his eyes caught site of a folder sticking out of her briefcase, causing him to chuckle. Of course it was emerald green. Man, they were good with their branding. His gaze darted to the bed they'd shared but instantly flew back to the folder.

Wait a minute. He'd seen that folder before. Where? Chad's Jeep? No, that wasn't it.

"Shit!" He knew exactly where he'd seen one just like it.

Flying across the room, he threw on his pants, not bothering to put on his shirt. He grabbed for the notepad and pen on the nightstand, scribbled a quick note, and set it on Ashley's pillow.

Convincing her that what had happened between them last night was a good thing would have to wait. He needed to call his boss.

CHAPTER ELEVEN

Ashley stood behind the tea bar, pouring both Emerald Morning and Cherry Berry Spice iced tea in sample paper cups and chatting with exhibit attendees. It was the last morning of the expo and all in all, the week had been a resounding success. Soon she'd be breaking down her exhibit and catching an evening flight back to Seattle.

Pride overwhelmed her inside, knowing that thousands of attendees had stopped by her exhibit even in the back of the hall.

Except for one.

Jacob had kept his distance since they'd slept together. He'd stopped by each morning to check in on her and then disappeared for the rest of the day. Though he made it a point to call her in the evenings to say good night, he didn't appear interested in another round in her bed.

Fine by her. She'd been the one who wanted to go back to normal, after all. Normal meant they hated each other and stayed out of each other's way.

She sighed and reached into her skirt pocket for the note Jacob had left on her pillow. There wasn't anything normal about the way her stomach continued to twist every time she read his words.

I have always been crazy about you, Ashley Whitman. That is the truth. —Jacob

Truth?

If that were true, why was he going around pretending like what they'd done hadn't even happened? Maybe he regretted what they had done and had been caught up in the moment when he'd written it.

She knew she had her own set of trust issues after the heartbreak and pain her mom had inflicted on her dad. If he'd always been crazy about her, then why was he always so quick to trade insults? That seemed juvenile.

She reached for a tea cup. Could Jacob have had these feelings for her all these years and she never realized it? She certainly didn't have a good track record in reading men.

"Hey, Ash." Graham sauntered over, causing her to quickly fold the paper and tuck it back in her pocket.

Speaking of which.

She never bothered asking Graham about the brunette he had been entertaining in the bar. After sleeping with Jacob, did she really have any right?

They'd had dinner last night in the hotel where he'd attempted to kiss her goodnight in the elevator. She'd hit the button to open the doors before his lips reached hers, aborting his attempt.

She was no longer interested in Graham romantically. Her heart hadn't quite sorted out her feelings to start publicly broadcasting she was on Team Jacob, but she could no longer deny their chemistry. No, not after what they shared. How she felt about the deputy was way stronger than any feelings she'd had for Graham.

"Hi," she greeted him.

"Everything going okay?" Graham asked, flashing a smile.

"Couldn't be better." She grabbed a tea cup and set it in front of him. "Tea?"

"Whitman tea? Would love some."

"Hot or cold?" she asked.

"The hotter the better." He slid onto the barstool. "I'm sorry we haven't been able to spend any time together this week."

"I understand. We've both been busy." *Sleeping with other people …*

She looked down at the steaming tea in his cup. No bubbles. That had to be a sign. "Here's the Emerald Morning, one of our most popular blends. Careful, it's hot."

Taking a quick sip, he pulled the cup back and pinched his lips. "Hmmm … delicious. There's something unique in it, what is it?"

"Like I'd tell a competitor," she kidded.

"So, where's your bodyguard?"

She shrugged. "I don't know. Ever since the incidents back home with my dad and the visitor's center, he's been preoccupied. He hasn't been around much." That sounded so much better than the reason she feared Jacob was avoiding her: He regretted what they'd done.

Graham arched an eyebrow. "Do they have any leads?"

"No, not really. Jacob said something about a possible suspect, but he couldn't really talk about it."

"Interesting …" Graham glanced around and waved to someone near the main stage. "I've got to help greet the VIPs for lunch. You good here?"

"Very. Thank you."

"I'll see you later."

"See you." Ashley waved and went back to engaging with her attendees. She'd met so many great people and a number of potential new suppliers. No sooner did she wrap up another tea tasting when Jacob sauntered up to the bar.

"Hey."

"Hey," she repeated and busied herself, restocking her plastic teacups. It didn't go unnoticed that he looked incredibly sexy in his casual, dark jeans and black polo shirt. She took a deep breath, trying her best to suffocate the butterflies in her stomach.

It didn't work. Apparently, a whiff of his cologne was all they needed to multiply. She should have known.

"Can you take a break?"

"Why?"

"We need to talk." He paused and tilted his head toward the exit. "Outside."

Ashley studied his demeanor. He seemed rushed and a bit preoccupied. "Okay. Let me grab my purse and tell the estheticians I'm stepping out."

Seconds later, Jacob motioned for her to follow him as he exited the exhibit hall. He walked a few feet in front, leading her to an outside terrace.

A warm wind rustled through her hair as she breathed in the delicious sea salt air. If only she'd had some downtime to spend on the beach. It would have been nice also to see some of the city. Maybe take a trip across the border.

"How's your mom?" Jacob asked.

"You brought me out here to ask about my mother?"

"No … not really."

"She's fine. Stuart begged her to come home and she drove back to Los Angeles. I didn't even see her the next day. She sent me a text."

"I'm sorry." His sympathetic expression touched her, but it was really unnecessary. She and her mother would never have a close relationship. They probably wouldn't see each other again anytime soon.

"And your dad … how's he doing?"

Ashley cocked a curious eyebrow. Why the interest in her parents? "He's fine, too. I talked to him this morning, and he felt good enough to go to work. What is this really about, Jacob? Because I know you didn't drag me out here to get an update on my family."

He smiled. "Look … I know things have been weird since the other night."

"Just a little." She stepped closer to the ledge to look out onto the beautiful bay. It gave her little comfort, but she wasn't sure she wanted to have this conversation right now. Not when she didn't understand what she was feeling or how he felt, for that matter.

He came up beside her. "I have to go back to Emerald Springs, but I need a favor."

"What? You're leaving now?"

"Yes, my flight leaves in two hours, but don't worry. I've asked the convention center's lead security officer to keep an eye on the exhibit. I've also arranged for car service to take you to the airport." He pushed off the wall. "You'll be in good hands."

I thought you were on my flight for later tonight. What happened?"

"Change of plans. Your car's at SEA-TAC, right?"

"Yeah."

"I need to borrow it."

"But how will I get home?" she asked.

"I'll pick you up."

Ashley shook her head. "Well, that doesn't make any sense. Why can't you just ask your sister or Chad to come get you?"

"Please just do this." He reached up and massaged her cheek with his thumb, causing her heart to pound hard against her chest. Car keys, purse, her body—if he touched her again like that, he could have it all.

"Fine." She reached inside her purse and pulled out her keys. "You're lucky Graham's staying a couple days to wrap up, otherwise you'd have to take him home, too."

"Guess I lucked out." He shoved her keys in his pocket. "What time do you land tonight?"

"Not until 10 p.m."

"Great. I'll be there." He took off for the doors to go back inside.

"Typical," she called out.

He turned. "Excuse me."

She threw her hands up in the air. "You always run away, Deputy. Leave me standing here."

"What are you talking about?"

"Oh, I don't know—after arresting me, Chad's diner, the mud bath … and let's not forget the night before your infamous three-pointer where you crashed into me outside of the locker rooms, made one of your usual cheap shots about my legs, and then barreled into the gym."

His eyes danced with amusement. Oh, God. She had tipped her hand. Why did she go on and bring up high school? It bugged her that he'd held onto their picture all these years yet had given her the cold shoulder the last couple days after she found it. Did he finally get what he wanted and was ready to cast her aside?

Well, he didn't have the newspaper clipping anymore. He'd left it on her nightstand, and it now had a new home in her purse.

"You know, you're absolutely right. I did forget something that night all those years ago.

Something I should have done on the basketball court, at the diner, and in the mud bath; something that probably wouldn't have been appropriate at the station; and something I can't wait to do right now."

"What?" She challenged him as the wind whipped through her hair.

With a couple of quick strides he was back at her side, spinning her into his arms. He raised her chin and kissed her softly at first, then deepened it. His tongue played with hers for a few seconds before he broke the kiss. "Nice legs."

"Too bad they'll never be around you … again," she murmured while gripping his shirt.

He grabbed her hands, threading his fingers through hers. "We'll talk about that when you get back."

With that, he took off inside the convention center, leaving her standing alone once again, but this time with tingling lips and a huge smile.

CHAPTER TWELVE

Jacob hit the Audi's accelerator down on the back roads of Emerald Springs. A man on a mission, he needed to pay a visit to his sister.

He'd called his boss once he left the airport, and they formulated their game plan. His fellow deputies had been secretly watching Carlos the last couple of days. What happened tomorrow would determine their next move.

And when Graham returned from San Diego, they'd be waiting for him. That is, if they had enough evidence to bring him in.

It had all come down to that emerald green folder in Ashley's room. The same color folder that Graham had given Carlos outside The Rusty Tap. Jacob had no doubt that Graham was behind the sabotage of Whitman properties and the contents in the folder were Richard's missing IRS paperwork he'd included in his statement after the phony immigration office visit. He just needed to prove it.

He glanced down at a black hair band wrapped around the console. Pulling it up, he wrapped it around his wrist, the goodbye kiss with Ashley still on his mind. He couldn't wait to turn her car around and pick her up later tonight.

He was sick and tired of being second to jerks like Graham. To hell with him being a Sanders and her being a Whitman. He was, for once in his life, going after what he wanted.

He'd asked to borrow her car so he could make sure it hadn't been tampered with. If Graham was behind the sabotage, it would be very easy to target Ashley next. No one would suspect that he'd do something malicious to her, given how close they'd gotten while working on the Tea Expo. Thank God that was over. Jacob would be keeping Ashley far away from that scumbag, if he had to follow her around twenty-four seven.

Not that he'd mind that job. When the timing was right, he planned on telling her everything. That he'd always had feelings for her, as far back as he could remember. Then he'd deal with the aftermath. If she wasn't in to him, he'd move on.

But her kiss goodbye certainly suggested otherwise.

Turning the corner, he drove into Split Acres, parked next to Colleen's truck, and headed straight for her office. "Hi, Kate," he greeted his sister's secretary with a huge smile. A loyal employee, she'd been with the farm for years and still baked him chocolate chip cookies from time to time.

"Hey, handsome. Colleen said you were coming over. How was San Diego?"

"You heard?"

"That you spent five days alone with Ashley Whitman? Who hasn't?"

"I wouldn't say we were alone. There were thousands of tea nuts."

She laughed. "How did that go?"

"Not bad." *The night in Ashley's bed was off the charts.* He smiled while his racing heart responded to that memory. "Not bad at all."

The door to Colleen's office flew open, and his sister motioned him in. She moved behind her desk and sat down, resting her hands on her stomach above her powder blue sundress. Jacob still couldn't believe he'd be an uncle before the year was out.

"Hey."

"Hey, back. Why do we need to meet?"

"Nice to see you." He took a seat. "How was my trip? Just fine. Thanks for asking."

That got a smart aleck grin. "Where are my manners?" she asked smugly. "Did you have a lovely time drinking tea with Ashley Whitman?"

"You know, Dad may have been wrong all those years ago. There are thousands of tea enthusiasts who can't get enough of the stuff."

She snorted. "Whatever. So, little brother, why did you insist we meet today—because I know you didn't come over to talk about tea."

"Well, in a way I did." He stood and shut her door. "I want to talk about Carlos."

"Carlos, my custodian. What about him? He's not in any sort of trouble, is he?" Her hand flew up and she massaged her temple. "Christ, that's all I need."

Jacob filled her in on Graham and what he saw outside The Rusty Tap, how the two men had exchanged a folder similar to the green folders the Whitmans used. "We've been tailing him the last couple of days."

"And has he done anything?"

Jacob shook his head. "No, nothing out of the ordinary. So far, when he's not here, he's been going straight home."

She reached for her phone.

"What are you doing?"

"Calling Alan. We'll fire that weasel and get his ass out of here."

"Not so fast."

"Why the hell not?"

"Well, we're still gathering proof." He paused. "We might have a witness."

"Who?"

"Sam Whitman."

"Sam?"

"He was jumped earlier this week after the Emerald Tea Farm visitor's center was vandalized."

"Oh crap." Her face filled with concern. "Do you think Carlos did it?"

Jacob shrugged. "It's possible. I've asked Sam to meet you here tomorrow."

"Why?"

"Because we don't want to tip off Graham and Carlos that we suspect anything. I need you to arrange for Sam to see Carlos. He works on Saturdays, right?"

"Yeah, but …"

"Sam's more than willing to help. He has some doctor appointments today, but he promised to stop by first thing in the morning. If he recognizes Carlos as the man who jumped him, we'll bring him in for questioning."

Colleen shook her head. "I don't like this one bit. What if he's also the guy behind all the crazy things that happened here this spring?" She stood and looked out her window. "But that couldn't be. We only hired him just last month, and he's not from around here."

"Doesn't mean he wasn't already in Emerald Springs."

"True." She sighed. "So when should I expect Sam?"

"10:00 a.m. I want to make it look like he's a friend dropping by."

That got an eye roll. "Sam and I friends? Yeah right." She turned and sat back down. "Fine. I'll pretend I'm showing him around the new greenhouses for his paper column. Alan can ask Carlos to tidy them up at nine thirty."

"Perfect." Jacob glanced down at his watch. He wanted to go into the station and go over all the evidence with a new eye. "I'll call you later this evening." He headed to the door.

"Jacob," Colleen called out. "You're playing with some seriously screwed up individuals who have gone great lengths to hurt the Whitmans, not to mention what they did to this farm. Are you sure you want to handle this case?"

He smiled and tugged on Ashley's elastic hairband still around his wrist. "More than you know."

• • •

Ashley stepped off the plane and headed to baggage claim. Jacob had sent her a text that he'd be waiting for her there. Sure enough, when she arrived at her carousal he stood with his back to her. She cocked her head, enjoying the view. He hadn't changed from earlier, and the memory of clinging to that polo after he'd kissed her silly made her smile.

It was nice to be home. After he'd left her, she'd greeted the last few attendees and then helped the convention staff break down the exhibit before heading to the airport. Graham was nowhere to be found, but she suspected he was busy wrapping up himself. It didn't really bother her that they hadn't said goodbye.

She didn't know where this thing with Jacob was headed, but she was eager to find out. What would it be like for a Whitman and Sanders to date? It wasn't like the families were feuding—well, other than Joe and Richard not speaking. None of her cousins would bat an eye, and she was pretty sure Zoe would do cartwheels.

He turned and her heart melted.

What was this man up to? "Hi, are those for me?" She pointed to the red and white pompoms in his hand.

"I thought we could start over, and I could redeem myself." He handed them to her.

She gave her familiar old friends a shake. "You want me to cheer?"

"Not exactly." He hoisted her up just as he had done all those years ago.

"Jacob what are you doing?" She dropped the pompoms and slid her hands down his muscular arms, falling into his embrace.

"Welcoming you home." His lips touched hers, softly at first, and then he deepened the kiss. "Welcome home," he murmured into her hair.

Minutes later, they headed out of the airport to her car. What a greeting. If she was having any doubts how he felt about her, they were extinguished now. Arriving at her car, Jacob popped the trunk and lifted her suitcases in.

"That was quite a welcome, deputy."

"There's more where that came from." He winked and offered her her keys. "Want to drive?"

She looked down at his hand. "No, I think I'll let you take me home. I mean, to your home." She was sure her blush matched the pompoms she still held in her hand. "Where did you get these? Because I know Colleen wasn't a cheerleader."

"I'm the town's beloved deputy. I know people." He laughed. "Who know people." He smiled down at them. "Patty helped me."

"Oh, my gosh. Are these really mine?"

"Yep. Patty said they were in the attic on the farmhouse along with Chad's old baseball glove and Adam's track trophies."

"That's so cute." She shook the pompoms. "Go Cardinals."

The drive back to Emerald Springs went by quickly, where they mostly talked about the expo and how her dad was doing. Within no time, Jacob pulled into his small, two-story ranch house in town.

She remembered hearing he'd decided to buy something recently but had forgotten that he'd lived on one of the cutest streets in Emerald Springs, with its curvy road and lush trees.

He shut off the engine and twisted toward her. "Want to come in?"

Hell, yeah!

She shrugged. "Maybe for a minute."

• • •

Jacob tried to contain the excitement bursting through him. Never in his wildest dreams did he think he'd be entertaining Ashley in his home, but here she was and by the subtle glances and touches she'd given him the whole car ride home, they were about to repeat the night they had in San Diego.

He flipped on the light and held the door open for her and bowed. "Welcome to my *casa, senorita*."

She grinned. "Do all the ladies get this kind of greeting?"

"I haven't had many guests since I moved in." He chuckled. "Except for my sister."

"What about Kimi?"

Taking her hand, he led her to the kitchen. "What about her?"

"Well, weren't you two close?"

"No, not really." He switched on the light.

"Could have fooled me," she said, rubbing her fingers along his kitchen island.

Well, how about that. He tilted his head and studied her. Kimi had been right that day about a pretty, blonde voyeur. It was time to bust her. "You saw us at the airport, didn't you?"

"I have no idea what you're talking about."

Yes she did, and her jealousy was so hot.

Ashley pointed to the rack his pots and pans hung from. His mom had helped with the décor, insisting the kitchen needed to look like it was used.

"Do you cook much?"

"Nah … But I make an awesome chili. What about you?"

"I'm pretty good in the kitchen."

"Yeah? What do you like to make?"

She leaned back on the island. "All sorts of things. But dessert's my favorite dish." Her suggestive smile was all he needed.

They could spend tonight trading recipes or they could get cooking. He preferred the latter.

"So, Jacob. I've been thinking." She paused and he hung on her next words. "I'd like for you to show me."

"Show you what?"

"These deep feelings you apparently have for me."

He yanked open his refrigerator, peering in. She'd probably prefer wine, but he was more of a beer guy. He had some of Chad's recent brew in the front. Loved that his buddy kept his refrigerator stocked. Hopefully that wouldn't change once the microbrewery was up and running. He twisted off the cap and handed the bottle to Ashley.

"Deep feelings? I don't know what you're talking about." He loved where this conversation was headed, and soon it would conclude in his bed. Still, he was enjoying the buildup and teasing her a bit.

She took a sip. "So, you don't have strong feelings for me?"

"Nope. Hate to disappoint you. I got caught up in one of those … what are they called? Shipboard romances."

"I see. You just happened to carry a picture of us from ten years ago in your wallet because …"

"Should I remind you, winning that game was a personal highlight."

She smirked. "And you told me I peaked in high school. Looks like you did, too."

Reaching out, he tapped his bottle to hers. "To us reaching our peak."

She set her bottle down and then his, grabbing his hand. "Solve this mystery, Deputy Sanders. Do you always wear women's hair ties around your wrist?" Pulling it off, she threw it around her hair and curled her ponytail around her finger. He knew what those fingers could do curled around a certain lower area on him. This game was over.

"Busted." He hoisted her up onto the kitchen island. The best use of this counter since he moved in, as far as he was concerned. Her legs instantly wrapped around him. "Glad you changed your mind about these." He ran his hands up each leg, ready to rip her jeans off.

"Me, too." She brought her beautiful, full lips close to his. He couldn't hold back any longer, and neither could she as their mouths joined and tongues lashed. In the back of his head, he thought he heard a noise out front but ignored it. It was probably the neighbors coming home. They liked to go out on Friday nights.

"Oh, hell no!"

Jacob stepped back to see his sister standing in the hallway connecting the living room and kitchen, hand over her eyes.

Ashley buried her head in his chest. "Hi, Colleen," she mumbled.

"I'll be in the living room." His sister did an about-face. "Jacob, get your butt in here."

Jacob rubbed Ashley's back, stifling a laugh. "It will only be a minute." He kissed her nose. "Stay right here."

Ashley nodded. "Right. Probably a good idea." She giggled. "But then I want your butt back here." She nodded to the stairs. "Then maybe up there."

He moved to the living room. This better be good. Why would his sister pay him a visit at this hour? Surely she wasn't here to raid his refrigerator for a midnight craving. He laughed as Colleen paced the room, clutching one of his billy clubs. "Um … you want to put that down and tell me what you're doing here?"

"What in God's name are you doing?" she asked, pointing the club directly in his face. A former lacrosse player, she knew how to use a stick.

He chuckled. "Given your condition, I kind of think you know what we were about to do before you so inconveniently interrupted."

"Have you lost your freakin' mind?"

"Okay. Calm down." He eased the baton out of her hand. "Why don't you tell me why you're here. It's nearly midnight."

She lowered her voice. "I just wanted to tell you that your princess's daddy didn't recognize Carlos."

Jacob raised an eyebrow. "Sam was at the farm today?"

"Yeah, he stopped by shortly after you left. Said plans had changed and today was a better day for him."

"Why didn't he call me?" He raked his hands through his hair. "Okay, what happened?"

"Nothing. We …" She brought her hand up in air quotes. "'accidentally' ran into Carlos in the fields. Sam said later that he definitely wasn't the guy. The asshole that attacked him wasn't Latino."

"Interesting."

"So what should I do about Carlos? Alan's ready to fire him."

"Not yet. Tell you what. I'll talk to the sheriff tomorrow about bringing him in for questioning. How about you and I connect first thing in the morning."

"We better. If something is going on, I want that ass off my property." She spun around in her rain boots. "Is this leftover in the kitchen something you'll throw out later?"

He chuckled at his sister's way with metaphors. "That amazing woman in there might prove to be the best thing that has ever happened to me." Jacob walked his sister to the door and kissed her goodbye. "Drive safe." He paused, his eyes crinkled in amusement. "And next time, please call. I don't need Alan reading me the riot because you're running around at midnight."

She rolled her eyes but took the hint. Minutes later, he strolled back into the kitchen. Ashley was gone. A note lay on the counter where she had sat.

Jacob Sanders, I'm waiting. Show me how much I drive you crazy.
Ash

He locked up and turned off the downstairs lights, knowing his guest had made herself at home.

Racing up the steps, he stopped in his bedroom doorway. A rush went through him as he enjoying the sight on his bed. "I see you've made yourself comfortable."

Ashley wore his deputy hat and nothing else. With his white sheet suggestively wrapped around her middle and her bare arms and legs exposed, she tugged on his handcuffs. "I thought we could use these again," she suggested coyly. "Maybe on you this time."

Jacob slowly moved to the bed and removed his hat, pulling out her hair tie and slipping it back around his wrist. He'd meant what he said to Colleen. This thing with Ashley could possibly be the best thing that ever happened to him. Taking the handcuffs, he flung both to the floor. "Maybe next time."

He lowered his head and kissed her neck, breathing in her delicious perfume. "Right now, I want to show you how much you mean to me. No pompoms and no handcuffs."

And with every touch, kiss, and caress that's exactly what he did.

CHAPTER THIRTEEN

Ashley stood, mouth agape. Her dad's recount of what had happened had no way prepared her for the amount of damage before her. Her beautiful visitor's center was now a cold, empty warehouse. Gone was the tea bar and neatly organized shelves that showcased Emerald Tea products. Stripped were the bright local artists' paintings that she'd lovingly hung along the walls. It looked like it had before she transformed it: a sterile warehouse devoid of life.

Adam joined her inside, resting a comforting hand on her shoulder. "I thought you might stop in here first."

She sighed, bringing her paper coffee cup up to her lips. "Why is this happening to us?"

"That is the million dollar question. Let's go up to the offices and talk." He waved the brown bag in his hand. "Zoe sent blueberry muffins to celebrate your return."

Somehow she wasn't sure even her best friend's amazing muffins could cure her heartbreak. She followed Adam outside and up to the farmhouse, fighting the urge to turn around and rush back to the visitor's center. She'd worked so hard on creating a welcoming experience for their buyers, suppliers, and guests. And now, poof, it was gone.

What kind of malicious individual would do this? All of her wonderful plans to bring customers in this fall and during the holidays would surely be delayed if not outright canceled. She sighed. Her tea bar always looked so cute strung up with garland and red bows.

"Have you talked to your dad?"

She nodded. "I stayed at his house this weekend. It looks like his eye is healing; he doesn't seem to be in any pain."

"Excellent."

"He told me to tell you he won't be in today but will be back with a vengeance tomorrow."

Adam chuckled, jamming his hands in his pocket. "I don't doubt it."

"I'm taking him to his follow-up appointment with Dr. McDonald later this afternoon. I hope it's okay if I cut out a little early."

"He needs you to drive?"

"No. I just know he'll blow it off if I don't personally escort him."

Adam nodded in agreement. "Your dad and mine are similar that way. Stubborn to a fault."

"Must run in the Whitman blood."

"Determination does, too." He patted her back. "I heard San Diego was a tremendous success."

"Thank you. It was." Ashley reached in her briefcase to pull out some summary reports she'd generated yesterday while her dad slept. His cozy home office overlooked Lake Emerald and was the perfect place for inspiration. "I have lots of great things to fill you in on."

"Sounds good." They reached the farmhouse, and Adam held the door open for her. "Have you seen Jacob since you've been back?"

That was an understatement. She'd seen quite a bit of him Friday night and most of Saturday morning before leaving his house to go to her dad's.

"He picked me up at the airport." She tried to downplay it but couldn't help smiling at the memory of him waiting for her with those silly pompoms. Jacob was quite the romantic.

"That's nice."

Taking a sip of her coffee, she followed Adam to his office.

"So there was no hair pulling?"

A little of the hot liquid flew out of her mouth and she coughed. "What do you mean?" she asked innocently.

"I remember how you two used to fight with each other growing up. I'm just looking out for you."

"Right …" Her cheeks might now be as bright as the red skirt she had on. "We got along just fine." *And there definitely was hair pulling.*

"So Ashley. I need to ask you something."

"What's up?"

"How well do you know Graham Carpenter?"

• • •

Jacob walked up the wooden steps to the Whitman farmhouse and entered. After all these years, it was still weird to see that much of it had been converted into offices, and he wouldn't be greeted by either Sheila or Patty with a cookie.

So many Sundays after church had been spent here playing with Colleen and all the Whitman kids before the fallout between his father and Richard. What would it have been like if the feud had never happened?

Adam told him on the phone earlier his office was the first one on the right, so Jacob headed directly for it. He could hear Ashley's voice from inside and paused, not sure if he should interrupt.

"Not as well as I thought," she said. "Graham came down a few times to work on the expo. We had dinner at Blush and Emerald Eats a couple of times."

They'd had dinner together. His fists clenched just at the thought. Man, he wanted to wring that prick's neck. Even if she no longer had feelings for the creep, Ashley was going to go ballistic when she learned the truth.

But what was the truth? Sam saying Carlos wasn't his attacker had been a major setback. He continued to listen.

"Was Graham ever on the farm?" Adam asked and Jacob's ears perked up.

"No, we always met at Daniel's resort or at a restaurant. Why do you ask?"

Jacob cleared his throat. He didn't want Adam to inadvertently tip her off that Graham was their lead suspect. Not yet. Ashley was smart as hell and would easily put two and two together.

Adam looked up from his desk and waved him in. "Hi, Jacob."

Ashley stood. "Deputy." She flashed her gorgeous smile in his direction.

He cocked his hat. "Ms. Whitman. Nice to see you."

She sauntered out of Adam's office and he suspected the toss of her gorgeous mane before she disappeared down the hall was for his benefit. He'd confessed to her in his bed how he could spend hours running his fingers through it.

Though she'd spent the last two days with her dad, he hoped they'd have more alone time this week. Maybe he could take her out to dinner even. Though he wouldn't take her to Blush or Emerald Eats or anywhere she'd gone with Graham, at least not for their first dinner date.

"Thanks for coming by. Have a seat." Adam motioned for Jacob to take Ashley's vacated chair while he closed his door. "Dad will be joining us any minute."

"No problem." Jacob sat and glanced around the spacious office. Adam's UCLA diploma hung on the wall, while a framed picture of Zoe was prominently displayed on his mahogany desk.

It looked like Adam had settled into his new role. Good for him. Jacob had always liked and respected Adam for the choice he made not to stay in Emerald Springs but to venture out on his own and do something unexpected all those years ago.

A move that sometimes Jacob wished he'd had the guts to do. His father never expected him to run Split Acres; it could have been very easy for Jacob to leave and never look back.

But he knew why he hadn't left Emerald Springs, and the reason was down the hall.

They'd had a great weekend in his bed, but were they a couple? That was the question. They hadn't done much talking in between their lovemaking. He just couldn't resist taking what he'd always wanted again and again when she gave it to him without hesitation.

He shifted in his seat. Now was not the time to reminisce about his time in bed with the blonde Whitman.

"Care for some …" Adam walked toward a small table near the window, holding a pitchers and glasses. "Water?"

Jacob snickered. "For a second, I thought you were going to offer me tea."

"No, I suspect you had enough of that last week. I heard things went well."

"Yeah, no incidents, but …"

"But what?"

"It's like I said on the phone. I can't prove it yet, but I believe Graham Carpenter is behind all of it, and Ashley has unintentionally been feeding him information."

Adam shook his head. "I've never met the guy, but to think that a competitor would sabotage us …" He paused. "I thought that kind of stuff only happened in the movies. Certainly not here in Emerald Springs."

Jacob leaned back. That first menacing act certainly did seem to be taken right out of a film script. Immigration officers had paid a visit four months ago under the guise of suspecting illegal hiring activity with the farm's field workers. Adam had been smart to follow up with the immigration office. Otherwise, who knew if they'd have ever learned that those officers had been imposters.

Now the question on his mind was had Graham hired two thugs to pose as the officials? That federal offense could lock him away for years.

A quick knock at the door preceded Richard's arrival. Jacob stood. "Hello, Mr. Whitman."

"Hello, son. Glad to see my niece didn't rip you to shreds last week."

Oh, didn't she. His uniform concealed the evidence on his back. "No, we got along great, sir."

Adam motioned for his dad to take the empty chair next to Jacob. "Dad, we were just talking about the real possibility of Graham Carpenter being the one behind the mayhem."

"I still can't believe it. Since Adam told me about your suspicions last night, Jacob, it's all I've thought about. Seattle's Pure Tea does fine on their own. Do they have the notoriety of Whitman? No, but they've only been around for five years or so. Why in God's name would Graham want to destroy us?" He paused. "Or Split Acres."

Jacob twitched at Richard's afterthought. The senior Whitman would always see the Sanders farm as small potatoes.

"Have either of you ever met Graham?"

Both Richard and Adam shook their heads.

"No, never dealt with him," Richard said. What kind of proof do you have that he's behind it?"

"Well …" Jacob started out slowly, choosing his words wisely. "Right before I left for San Diego, I saw him outside The Rusty Tap. He appeared to be meeting up with one of my sister's farm custodians named Carlos."

"The guy you were hoping Uncle Sam could identify as his attacker?" Adam asked.

"That's the one. When I saw him talking to Graham outside the bar, naturally, I thought it was odd." He leaned over and grabbed a folder lying on Adam's desk. "Graham passed Carlos one of these."

Adam's eyes widened. "You don't think he was giving him Dad's missing paperwork, do you?"

"That's exactly what I think. I only realized it was one of your branded Emerald Tea Farm folders when I saw a similar one that Ashley had in San Diego."

"And you think?" Richard asked, his voice trailing.

"I think your missing IRS papers were what he passed to Carlos and probably a payoff to get rid of them."

Richard flew off his chair and began to pace. "Adam, I knew I didn't lose that folder."

Jacob nodded. "But there's a problem. I didn't mean to eavesdrop, Adam, but I overhead Ashley saying he's never been to the farm."

Adam agreed. "That does put a wrinkle in your theory, doesn't it?"

Richard sat down. "That must mean the weasel broke in after hours, stole the folder, and then sent up the phony immigration officials to come out here."

"It's possible," Jacob said.

"So what are you going to do, deputy?" Richard asked. "How soon can you toss this low life's butt in the slammer and throw away the key?"

Jacob smiled. So this is who Ashley had gotten her flare for drama from. Richard certainly had it in spades. "There's the little matter about this last incident."

"Graham was in San Diego," Adam replied, obviously knowing where Jacob was going.

"Exactly. As much as I'd like to pin everything that has happened on that asshole, Graham has a solid alibi, and Sam didn't recognize Carlos as his attacker."

Adam's eyebrows furrowed. "Wait. When did Sam see Carlos?"

"I arranged for him to stop by Colleen's where she made sure they ran into him. Sam was supposed to go over on Saturday, but he ended up visiting her on Friday afternoon. He didn't tell you?"

"No, but he's been a bit quiet since the attack. I didn't hear from him all weekend. Did you, Dad?"

Richard shook his head. "Not a peep. Figured he was resting and spending time with Ashley."

"You'd think he would have told one of us," Adam replied.

Richard shrugged. "My brother is all out of sorts these days. He probably thought he did and forgot. What about Daniel? Has he seen this Carlos?"

Jacob nodded. "I had Colleen take an employee shot for their website yesterday and e-mailed it over to him. He said Carlos could have been the man that punched him, but that the guy had on a ski mask so he couldn't say yes with certainty."

Adam placed his hand to his forehead. "Why is all of this happening now that I'm in charge?" His attempt at a joke got a small chuckle from his father.

"Welcome home," Jacob said.

"So, where does all of this leave us?" Richard asked.

Jacob leaned back and sipped his water. "Gentleman, I think there could be someone else working with Graham, besides Carlos, to gain access into Whitman properties, and we need to explore the possibility the person is an insider."

CHAPTER FOURTEEN

Ashley slid into the open booth opposite Zoe. They had finished one of their regular runs delivering baked goods and tea to the Emerald Springs Senior Day Center. Since they'd gotten a late start and it was nearly noon, Ashley suggested they grab lunch at Emerald Eats and catch up on wedding preparations.

Jacob breezed in, smiling at Ashley. "Ashley."

"Jacob." That was the second time today he'd greeted her so cordially in public. She was loving the little secret they shared—they and well, also Colleen, whose eyes were no doubt still burning from what she had walked in on.

"Oh, my God!" Zoe's slammed her menu down.

"What?" Ashley tossed hers to the side, craving one of Chad's yummy organic Cobb salads and a Diet Coke.

"You had sex with Jacob in San Diego."

"You're insane."

"Am I?" Zoe leaned forward, lowering her eyes. "Am I?"

Ashley shrugged her answer.

"I knew it!"

Ashley's finger went up to her lips to silence her best friend. Zoe could excite easily. "Shh … I don't want him to hear—or anyone else in this diner for that matter. That's all I need."

"So are you two seeing each other?"

"I think so." Ashley laughed at how silly that sounded. She really didn't know what they were doing but hoped they'd be doing more of it soon. Maybe she could invite him over for dinner one night this week and show off her mad cooking skills. "We really haven't talked about it."

Zoe clapped her hands. "How cute you both will look at my wedding." She paused. "Wait. What happened to Graham?"

"Let's just say, I realized quickly he wasn't the one for me." Her gaze shifted over to Jacob, who appeared to be in deep conversation with Chad. His sheriff's uniform was covering all the parts she couldn't wait to get her hands back on. Oh, the number she'd done on his poor back. He hadn't complained.

Before they continued whatever it was they were doing, they needed to talk. Sure, he'd shown her how much he'd always wanted her, but now that they'd had sex twice—okay, four times—would they be moving in the direction of full-fledged couple?

Was it even a good idea? Whitmans and Sanderses didn't exactly have a reliable track record of comingling.

The real question she struggled with: could she trust that Jacob wouldn't break her heart? They'd never gotten along—ever. Who was to say they wouldn't fall into their old pattern and go back to irritating each other once the novelty wore off?

The sex was incredible. She left his house Saturday morning content, happy, and a little sore, but it had been way better than any Zumba class she taught. The deputy definitely had moves.

The only thing they didn't do was talk. They tried, but every time they'd start to, his fingers would get lost in her hair or her hands would massage the spot that drove him crazy and all conversation would cease.

Was he even looking for more? He'd said he'd always been crazy about her, but what exactly did that mean?

Zoe's fingers snapping brought Ashley out of her thoughts. "What do you have planned for us this week?"

"Planned?" Ashley asked. A waitress arrived and set down their lunch.

"Um … you are my unofficial wedding planner. The wedding's in five weeks."

"Oh, right. Yes." She stabbed a crouton with her fork. Truth be told, she hadn't really thought about the wedding since she returned. "I'm sorry. With all that happened last week in San Diego and here, I'm a bit behind."

Zoe's hand went up in the air. "Does this mean I get to bake my cake?" she asked hopefully.

Ashley wiggled her nose. "No, it most certainly does not. Your cake has already been ordered, remember? We need to practice your hair and makeup. How does tonight sound?"

"Sure. Why don't you come over after work? We can grab Chinese food and you can tell me all about how good your deputy is in the—" Zoe stood abruptly. "Hi, Jacob. Take my seat and visit with Ashley. I'm sure you two have a lot to talk about."

Ashley widened her eyes, giving her friend the subtle hint to shut her mouth. "I'll see you tonight, Zoe."

"See you." She winked and rushed out the door.

Jacob took Zoe's seat. "Hi."

"Hi." She looked down at her salad. What was Chad going to say when he saw them sitting together? Sure, Colleen had caught them kissing, but was Ashley ready for her family to know?

It wasn't like she would be embarrassed to date Jacob. Their family feud had been ages ago. Still, how would she explain that her very public dislike for him since they were kids had suddenly turned into something romantic? Did that make her a hypocrite?

"Everything okay?"

"I saw the visitor's center today." She looked down at her salad. "It's completely destroyed."

"I know." He reached out and touched her hand. "I'm sorry. We'll get whoever did this. I promise." His hand now covered hers and its warmth gave her a sense of protection unlike anything she'd ever experienced.

"Well, look at you two." Chad approached, and Ashley instinctively pulled her hand away. "Did you bury the hatchet in San Diego?"

"The deputy was just filling me in on the investigation. That's all."

Chad took a seat next to Ashley. "Dude, did you nab the guy who beat up Uncle Sam?"

Jacob locked his eyes with hers. "That's what Ashley and I were just talking about. We thought we had a suspect, but Sam couldn't identify him," Jacob said.

"My poor dad." Ashley sighed. "I hate that he got caught in the crossfire. Who would beat up an old, defenseless man?"

"How's his eye?" Chad asked.

"Surprisingly, much better." She reached in her purse and pulled out her phone. "That reminds me, I'm waiting for him to check in. He had a doctor's appointment this morning. I wanted to take him, but he called an hour ago, insisting on going alone. Why is it men never want any help?"

Both Chad and Jacob stared at her, expressions blank. *Figures.*

Jacob looked down at his phone and stood. "I should get back to the station. I'll see you later?"

"Sure, man. Stop by the house tonight if you want. We can watch the game," Chad said.

Ashley slow blinked, knowing the question wasn't for her cousin. "See you, deputy."

Chad maneuvered across to the table, taking Jacob's seat while she picked up her fork and took another bite of her fabulous salad. Chad had a real talent for farm-to-table cuisine. "So, Chad, have you and Daniel planned Adam's bachelor party?"

"The groom is being a little difficult on that one."

"Zoe is the same way about her bachelorette party. Don't they want one last night of freedom?"

"Apparently not." Chad leaned back in the booth. "It really doesn't surprise me."

"Me, neither. They're both so anxious to get married."

"I've got an idea ... What if we did something here for both of them?"

"In the restaurant?"

"Yeah, we could close it for the night and turn this place into a little Vegas casino with games and music ..." He winked. "Great food and amazing beer."

His suggestion was intriguing. "That could be fun. We could designate one area for the girls and one for the fellas." She tapped her fingers on the table. "Maybe the ladies could get some spa pampering while the men play poker."

"Yeah, we could totally move some tables around and make it all work." He smirked. "Install some neon lights, bring in a couple of show girls."

She kicked his leg underneath the table. "No strippers."

"I can't make any promises." Chad stood. "Sounds like we've solved our dilemma. I should get back in the kitchen. Let's talk more this week and set the date. I'll fill Dan in on the plan, too."

After finishing her lunch, Ashley left the restaurant to head back to the farm. Chad's suggestion had triggered several ideas she wanted to run with at once. Adam and Zoe weren't the kind of couple that needed one last night to let their hair down at some club in Seattle. This way, all of their close friends and family could attend. Her dad, Uncle Richard, and Patty would even be able to stop by.

Ashley went to work mentally setting up an area in her head where she'd offer cocktails and makeovers. The more she thought about it, she loved this plan. It would make both hers and Chad's lives easier.

Hearing her phone vibrate in her purse, she reached for it. Hmmm, a text from her mother saying it was great to see Ashley last week. Well, that was nice.

Her gaze skipped across the street to the sheriff's station. Could she invite Jacob to the party? She didn't see why not. He was

Chad's best friend, after all. Maybe they could go public then that they were seeing each other.

A familiar SUV drove into the station parking lot, causing her eyebrow to shoot up. Seconds later, her dad jumped out and headed in. She started to cross the street to join him but hesitated. If it was about the attack, he might want some privacy.

What would her dad think once he learned that she and Jacob were a couple? He wasn't particularly a fan, often stating he thought Jacob was a bit on the lazy side and wouldn't make a good sheriff. Ashley suspected it had something to do with his being a Sanders.

Ashley got in her car and sighed. Eventually, she'd have to tell her dad about seeing her mother last week in San Diego and that she was dating Jacob. She wondered which news he'd take better.

• • •

Jacob went over his notepad for the umpteenth time. There had to be something that he and the other deputies weren't seeing. Until they figured it out, he wouldn't be able to bring Graham and Carlos in.

So much had happened the last few months: the immigration imposters and Richard's missing IRS paperwork, the tampered fence between the Whitmans' and Sanderses' properties that compromised the Whitmans' organic fields, the fire at Emerald Eats, the water damage at Emerald Paradise, and finally, the assaults on Daniel and Sam before the visitor's center destruction.

Then there were the odd things that happened at Split Acres: infected potato seeds, a fallen barn rafter, and the cement in Colleen's truck engine. If Graham and Carlos were behind the events plaguing the Whitmans, were they also behind what had happened to his sister? Carlos could have easily tampered with the potato crop, barn, and Colleen's truck. The question was why?

Were they hoping to rekindle the old Whitman/Sanders feud so that each would accuse the other of deliberately sabotaging their businesses?

Maybe that had been the original plan, but when it didn't work, they stopped messing with Split Acres and solely targeted the Whitmans?

And what did Graham have to gain? Running the Whitmans underground wasn't going to clear a path for Seattle's Pure Tea to be the leading tea producer in North America. According to Richard, they'd only been around a few years and weren't considered a real competitor. The Prevosts would have more to gain if the Whitmans ever did go under.

He hated telling his sister that they just didn't have enough evidence to bring Carlos in. That and trying to convince her that not firing Carlos would actually help them.

It'd be easier to keep an eye on him if they continued to pretend nothing was wrong. If she let him go, who knows where he'd run. No, they needed Carlos to stay exactly where he was for the time being and that meant Colleen not handing him a pink slip.

She had a few colorful words for him the first few minutes but then finally agreed after a little nudging from Alan. Jacob didn't know his brother-in-law very well, but every day he liked him more and more. Alan knew how to diffuse Colleen in ways that Jacob and his parents never could.

He glanced at the framed picture on his desk of his mom, dad, and Colleen posing with him when he became a deputy. He'd taken an oath to protect the citizens of Emerald Springs that warm, sunny day. He'd especially do anything he could to protect those he loved.

Including the woman his heart had recently added to the top of that list.

Would she even want his protection? Ashley's less-than-subtle removal of her hand when Chad joined them still on his mind. Was she embarrassed to be seen with him?

It hadn't bothered Jacob in the least when Colleen had caught them together. Hell, he admitted to his sister that Ashley could possibly be the best thing that ever happened to him.

But her pulling her hand away was harsh physical proof that they may not be on the same page.

Maybe she was having second thoughts.

He flipped to his notes from his conversation with Richard and Adam. Now was not the time to go all Dr. Phil on his love life.

A female deputy popped her head in the doorway. "Jacob, you have a visitor."

He looked up to see Sam Whitman standing behind her, hands shoved in his blue sports jacket. This was a surprise.

"Hi, Sam. Come on in." He motioned for him to take the empty seat across from his desk. Unlike the luxurious offices at Emerald Tea Farm, his tiny area screamed functional with an office table and two black metal chairs. He always joked if he did win a bid for sheriff, the first thing to go would be the uncomfortable chairs. "What brings you by?"

Sam took a seat. Ashley was right. His eye did seem to be healing rather quickly. Although, something was going on on the right side of his face. Tiny red bumps clustered around his cheek.

"Deputy, I'd like to talk to you about the investigation."

"Sure. Thanks for going out to Split Acres, by the way. I'm sorry Carlos wasn't the guy."

"You and me both." Sam shook his head. "It definitely wasn't him."

"So what's on your mind?" Jacob clicked his pen, prepared to take notes if he needed to.

"The guy that attacked me had bright, blue eyes. He had a mask on, but I got a good look at their color."

"Okay." Jacob jotted that down, disappointment running through him. That ruled out Carlos. They were back to square one.

"Well, while I was at Split Acres, I saw someone else who had the same blue eyes as the guy that jumped me." He paused. "You're not going to like it, but how well do you know your new brother-in-law?"

Jacob set his pen aside and stared at his visitor, refusing to break eye contact. "Sam, are you insinuating what I think you're insinuating?"

If Ashley's dad had nodded his head any faster, Jacob was pretty sure he'd get whiplash.

"I'd bet all the tea leaves in our fields that Alan was the one who attacked me."

CHAPTER FIFTEEN

Ashley grabbed her makeup case from her backseat, locked up her car in the general parking lot, and headed toward Zoe's bakery. It was almost time to meet the bride-to-be for an evening of sweet and sour chicken, great wine, girl talk, and makeup experiments.

It had been ages since they'd had a fun girls' night in. They'd often hang out at Ashley's condo or Zoe's apartment above the bakery, spending hours upon hours talking about their jobs, their love lives, and their families.

In a small way, she was sad to see their time hanging out above the bakery come to an end now that her friend would soon be moving into the house Adam had bought for them. A traditional romantic at heart, Zoe had decided to live in her apartment until she and Adam were married.

Although Ashley suspected there were many sleepovers at the new house.

She clutched her makeup case, not realizing how much she'd packed in it. Tonight would be fun. When it came to the big day, Ashley planned on having an amazing makeup artist in town do all of their faces, but tonight they'd play with her ideas.

The products in the case represented the first step in realizing her dream.

She strolled along Spruce Street, glancing over at the sheriff's station. Jacob's squad car sat in the parking lot. Soon, he'd head over to Chad's to drink some beer and watch the game. She grinned, reaching in her purse for her phone. Zoe wouldn't mind if she was a little late.

She crossed the street, texting Jacob that he needed to get his cute butt out to his car immediately. Then she hopped onto his hood, placing her makeup case next to her.

Within minutes, a grinning Jacob appeared—cute butt and all.

"Howdy, handsome." She tucked her red skirt underneath her, letting her bare legs dangle off the hood of his car.

"You know, I could arrest you for loitering on official sheriff's property," he said, hopping up next to her. "That would be twice in one month."

"Oh, but you didn't actually arrest me the first time," she pointed out.

"You've forgotten already?"

"No. You didn't read me my rights that day. I knew all along you were only messing with me."

"Yeah, right."

She smiled. "Okay, maybe Chad told me afterward."

"I've really got to talk to that pal of mine and remind him where his loyalty should lie." He laughed, pointing to her makeup case. "What's that?"

"My cosmetic collection."

He touched her face, sending her heart racing. "I'm flattered that you wanted to get dolled up for me, but you're most beautiful first thing in the morning."

She swatted him playfully, pretty sure her cheeks were red and now wouldn't need any of the blush she'd brought along. "If you must know, Zoe and I are getting together to practice her wedding face." She patted the case. "I've got enough in here to make her the woman of Adam's dreams."

"I think she already is."

"You're right, but she'll look absolutely stunning in my personal *A Touch of Ash* collection."

"A Touch of Ash?"

"I've been experimenting recently with tea foundations along with a makeup company in Olympia. They sent me some samples they whipped up using Emerald's green tea. I'd love to open my own line one day. Maybe sell exclusively to high-end resorts like Daniel's."

Jacob took her hand. "Ashley, that's awesome." Helping her off the hood, he brought his arms around her. "Have I told you how amazing I think you are?"

"I don't know if it's amazing. It's only makeup."

"No, don't sell yourself short." He touched her hair, looping a curl around his finger. "That's what I admire most about you. You're not afraid to go after what you really want."

"And you are?"

Leaning on his car, his shoulders hunched. "Sometimes I wonder if I have the balls to run for sheriff. What if I lose?"

"Jacob, everyone in this town loves you! You make us feel safe and secure and wanted."

"Wanted?" he asked, snickering.

She smiled. "Now, don't get cocky." She looked down at her watch. "I should probably go."

"I'll walk you over." He took a couple of steps, but stopped. "Unless you don't want me to."

"Why wouldn't I?"

He shrugged.

She studied his expression. Something was bothering him. Maybe it had something to do with work. "I know my dad stopped in today."

"Yes, he did."

"Everything okay?"

"Everything will be fine. I really shouldn't talk about it."

"Then we won't." She motioned for him to follow her across the street. They took the long way, detouring through the park. Jacob had a million questions about her makeup line. His interest in her passion excited her, and she wanted to know all about what he'd need to do to run for sheriff. Whatever was bothering him, he appeared to have put it aside.

He touched her arm while they waited at a crosswalk. "Ashley, you are amazing. Anything you decide to do, I know you'll be good at it."

"Why are you so confident?" she asked shyly, her arm all tingly from his touch.

"I've seen what you can do when you put your mind to it. Remember our fifth grade science project when you replicated Mt. Saint Helens erupting? Or what about the junior play you had the lead role in. Remember that standing ovation you got?"

Of course she did, but why did he? "You really did pay attention to me in school."

He lowered his eyes and she could tell he was embarrassed. "I noticed a few things, but not just back then. I also know you're a talented public speaker and can hold anyone's attention."

"I forgot you sat in on my tea presentation." She giggled. "What can I say? You speak the truth. God, I must have bored you to tears."

He smirked. "I'm really learning to like the stuff."

"You are?"

His inability to hold in his laugh gave his lie away. "Okay, I'm more of a coffee drinker, but I've been enjoyed some of the alternative uses for tea that I've experienced lately."

She shot an eyebrow up. "Care for another green tea mud treatment?"

"Only if you're going to be in there with me."

"I'll see what I can do." *Note to self: call Emerald Paradise and book the mudroom for an entire afternoon, STAT.* "Well, deputy. I know some things about you, too."

"You do?"

"I sure do. I know you love country music, still have a mean three-point shot, and know the names of virtually every pitcher in the National Baseball League."

"Wow, you did your detective work."

"Just call me Nancy Drew."

"Or Chad told you."

She laughed, knowing she was busted. "Okay, maybe he did, but I also know you're a great deputy who would do anything for this town."

"That I would," he said, growing serious.

"So what else have you noticed about me?"

"That you throw awesome shindigs on your farm, like Adam and Zoe's engagement party."

She nodded. "That was a great time. "If I remember right, you brought a date that night."

"I did?" He squinted his eyes.

"You seriously can't remember?" Oh, no. Was he confirming her worse fear? Not only did he like to play the field, he couldn't do something as simple as remember the name of the woman he'd called up to bat.

"No, I know. It was Andie Scott. I wouldn't exactly call it a date."

"You two weren't serious?" Was Jacob incapable of more than a good time?

"Not at all. We hung out a couple of times." He sighed. "I've never been very good at long term."

And there was her answer. Jacob was a player.

They were nearing the bakery, but she wasn't done with this conversation. If this thing between them was just sex, she needed to know. She led him to an empty bench next to a bus stop. "Jacob, I know we've had a couple of amazing nights."

"And …" He took a seat, wrapping his arm around her as two couples around their age stopped in front of them to wait for the bus.

She sat up, not letting his arm touch her. They were not going down this road. If he touched her again, she'd easily cancel plans with Zoe and spend the evening in his bed because that's what his touch did to her. She took a deep breath. This time, all they were going to do was talk. Period. "What is this?"

"What is this?" he repeated, moving his arm off the bench and cracking his knuckles. "What do you mean?"

"This thing between us." She bit her lip, ready for his answer. It didn't feel like it was just sex, but if it was, she'd deal with it.

"I don't know," he admitted.

"You don't know?"

"What is it to you?"

It was more than "I don't know," but she wasn't going to admit it since obviously he didn't feel the same way. She had way too much pride for that. "I don't know either."

They sat on the bench in awkward silence. Apparently a serious heart-to-heart wasn't going to happen now. Why had she gone over to the station in the first place?

Because she wanted to see him. Was that so wrong? If he knew how often she thought about him during the course of her day, would that completely freak him out?

She bit her lip, afraid she knew that answer, but hoping just maybe she was wrong. The walk through the park before she'd sprung the "what are we" question had been nice. He remembered so many of her accomplishments growing up. That had to mean something, right?

Maybe he just needed a little more time. "I should get going. I told Zoe I'd be there by seven. I don't want her going all bridezilla."

"I highly doubt she would lose her cool, but I should get over to Chad's, anyway."

"Yeah, wouldn't want you to miss out on your male bonding time with my cousin."

"Ash, thanks for texting me."

"You're welcome. Thanks for escorting me." She stood and smoothed her skirt. Maybe she shouldn't read too much into the last five minutes. Not just yet, anyway. It wasn't like either of them had any experience in talking with the other that didn't include trading insults … or tearing each other's clothes off, as of late.

They just needed more time to adjust to their new normal.

He reached again for her makeup case and grunted. The uncomfortable air between them disappeared and Jacob was back to his joking self.

"Oh, stop. It's not that heavy."

"Seriously, this is heavier than some of my weights."

"Shut up. The next big idea in beauty might be in there."

"I don't doubt it, but glad I won't be wearing any of it."

"Don't be so sure. I can be very convincing. Once Chad and I played dress up and he let me put eye shadow on him."

"No way."

"Yeah, don't tell him I told you." She laughed. "Oh and there was that time my dad participated in a local news interview when Uncle Richard was ill. I dabbed a little foundation on his face before he went on camera. He's so naturally pale."

"I'm sure your father loved that."

"Actually, he did … well, until his face broke out in a rash."

"Really? From the makeup?"

"Yeah, his skin is extremely sensitive. I think he gets that from my grandmother's side."

"Interesting …" his voice trailed.

What was so interesting about her dad's allergic reaction to a little foundation? They'd reached Zoe's bakery, but Jacob seemed to have already left her. "Thanks for the walk, deputy."

"Anytime." He shifted on his feet. She was pretty sure he'd pivot and run as soon as she said goodbye.

"Maybe we could finish our conversation tomorrow night?"

"Sure." He looked away. "Oh you know what. I promised Colleen I'd help her and Alan fix a tractor. I'll call you."

Her heart dropped to her stomach as he kissed her cheek and left her on the sidewalk. The peck felt obligatory and so different than the goodbye he'd planted on her in San Diego. That kiss had curled her toes.

"He needs to fix a tractor," she muttered, watching him sprint across the street. He'd rather get greasy under a piece of farm equipment than discuss their relationship?

If that wasn't a copout, she didn't know what was.

CHAPTER SIXTEEN

Jacob took a deep breath and entered the Coffee Queen. Inside, the aroma of freshly brewed coffee enticed his nostrils. He'd need it. He hadn't gotten much sleep last night after he'd left Ashley outside Zoe's bakery.

Hightailed it from her was more like it.

He just didn't know how to respond to her dinner invitation. He'd love nothing more than to spend time with her, but how would that conversation go? "Baby, I suspect your dad and the dipshit CEO of Seattle's Pure Tea might be working together to bring down Emerald Tea Farm. Would you like red or white wine?"

He hadn't a clue how to protect Ashley if his suspicions were right. She was very close with her father. He'd seen it firsthand in San Diego after she'd learned of his attack, not to mention her allegiance to him when her parents divorced.

How was she going to feel when she found out it was something she said that had tipped him off?

Jacob glanced around the restaurant, spotting his breakfast companion. That person was holding court, shaking customers' hands—mostly elderly patrons who enjoyed the early morning breakfast special the Coffee Queen offered. Just like a politician running for re-election, all he needed was a cute baby to kiss and he'd be all set.

"Hi, Dad," Jacob greeted his father.

"Jacob." His dad spun around. "Good to see you, son." He turned to the elderly couple he'd been chatting with. "This is your future sheriff in two years' time." He slapped Jacob on the back.

"Maybe three." Jacob smiled dryly and walked over to an empty table. He'd never been quite sure if his dad wanted him to run for sheriff because it would be good for Jacob's career, or if he just wanted at least one of his kids to have some real influence in Emerald Springs. Sometimes he suspected the latter. "See you are getting to know your constituents."

His dad laughed, taking a seat. "You'll have to do the same thing when you run for sheriff."

"*If* I run."

"You will." He nodded with conviction. "How are you?"

"Can't complain."

"Good. Your sister seems to be doing well."

One thing they could agree upon. "She and Alan are really turning things around. They'll have that place in the black in no time."

"Well, as long as she doesn't start harvesting tea leaves, I'm one hundred percent behind her." He put on his glasses and studied his menu. "What is good here besides coffee?"

"Their breakfast specials are a hit, loaded with bacon and eggs."

"Sounds good. Nice to enjoy breakfast without watching my cholesterol. Your mom has me on some kind of crazy diet she heard about from one of her yoga friends." He folded his menu. "So what's up? Why did you want to meet?"

Jacob glanced around, making sure there weren't any eavesdroppers. When he'd asked his dad to meet him at the Coffee Queen, he wasn't expecting such a crowd. This place might give Emerald Eats a run for their money.

He leaned in, ready to get this conversation started. "I'm seeing someone."

His dad threw his hands up in the air. "You had me drive two hours to talk about your love life? Couldn't you tell your mother over the phone?"

"No, I wanted to talk to you first," Jacob said.

"Why? Is she pregnant?"

Jacob laughed. Leave it to his dad to go there. Should he remind him that his darling Colleen was the one who got knocked up?

"No, she's not pregnant. I actually wanted to talk to you about her father."

"Who is it?"

"Sam Whitman."

"You're dating Ashley Whitman?" his dad asked, voice high.

"Yes, and I don't think the people in Seattle heard you."

"Sorry. Isn't she kind of high maintenance for you?"

"Not any more than I'm sure Mom is for you."

"Is it serious?" His father wore the same confused expression Colleen had when she walked in on them the other night.

"It could be." At least Jacob hoped so. Although his doubts grew even larger after the way she pulled away from him for the second time in public. It continued to gnaw at him that there was a real possibility she could be ashamed to be seen with him.

A waitress took their orders and filled their coffee cups. His father poured sugar into his and stirred.

"Ashley Whitman," his dad said. Disbelief all over his face. "Her mother's quite interesting."

"I know, right? I met her in San Diego."

"I heard you were doing something for Richard. It's about the things going on around town, isn't it?"

"Dad, you know very well I can't talk about it." It felt good for once to have the upper hand with his father. He also didn't want to worry him since Colleen hadn't shared with their parents the strange events that had happened at Split Acres, too.

"So what do you want to know about Sam? Does he not approve of you two dating?"

"I'm not sure he even knows yet." He took a deep breath, knowing the information his dad provided could be important, if not critical. "What was he like to work with when you and Richard were running WhitSand Farm?"

"Oh, son. That was so long ago." His dad took a sip of his coffee. "I don't live in the past."

"But surely you remember what Sam was like to work with." Hell, Jacob could recall everything he hated about his first boss working part-time at Annie's Arcade back in the day.

No, he knew his dad could tell him all about Sam; he just needed some encouragement. "I want to show Sam that Sanders men are just as good, if not better than the Whitmans. Knowing how he ticks could help me immensely."

That did it. His dad started talking.

"Well, back in the day, he wasn't a full-time employee but did marketing for us on the side while he got back on his feet."

"Back on his feet?"

"He had a fancy job at a big marketing firm in Seattle. He commuted daily for that. Within no time, he mucked it up and was fired. Richard felt sorry for him and gave him some marketing jobs to do for us here and there. Mostly flyers, advertisements in the *Emerald Springs Penny Saver*. That type of thing."

"When we dissolved WhitSand Farm and went our separate ways, Richard hired Sam full-time as his marketing director. Who the hell knows what he's really done all these years. I doubt Richard's ever given him any type of real responsibility."

"What about his temperament? Ever see him angry?"

His dad took a second before he spoke. "He's always been a bit flighty and quick to fly off the handle, especially when he didn't think Richard was listening to him, but then he'd go back to doing whatever it was he was told to do." The waitress brought over their breakfast and his dad dived in.

"Was Sam difficult to work with?"

"Nah ... but let me tell you, he's got a chip on his shoulder. He thinks the world owes him, and he's not above playing victim to get what he wants. I think his ex-wife messed him up when she ran off with a pool boy."

Jacob smiled. From the flashy jewelry she wore the night they'd had dinner, he highly doubted Ashley's mother would set her sights on anyone who fished for floating debris and tested chlorine. "I don't think it was actually a pool boy."

He shook his head. "I can't remember. All I know is that Sam gave that woman everything. Nice house on the lake, fancy car, membership to the country club before Emerald Paradise existed … anything she could ever want. It would be hard for any man to recover from that kind of rejection. Then there's his relationship with his brother …"

"Do you think it's contentious?" Jacob leaned in.

"Let's just say Sam always had a hard time playing second fiddle to Richard. I suspect he feels the same way about Adam now that he's in charge. I'm sure he hates taking orders from someone half his age. Some men aren't meant to go straight to the top, and Sam's one of them."

"Interesting," Jacob said.

They finished their breakfast and his dad motioned for the check. "I've got to head out. I want to go over to Split Acres and see with my own eyes some of these changes your sister's made before I head back to Olympia."

"Breakfast is on me." Jacob reached behind and pulled his wallet out his back pocket.

His father stood to leave. "Oh, and Jacob, dating Ashley could help your run for sheriff. As much as it kills me to admit it, the Whitman name stands out in this town. Keep that in mind."

"Right, sure, Dad," he said dryly. Of course his father would see Ashley as a pawn for net gain. He watched him leave, stopping at each table to shake hands and pass out "Vote for Joe" buttons.

Jacob scratched his day-old stubble. Had his father given him all the information he needed? Sam was a hot wire who never had fully gotten over what Elizabeth had done to him and felt inferior to Richard.

It was time to pay a visit to Emerald Springs hospital and finally confirm his suspicion.

•••

Ashley knocked twice on her father's office door and popped her head in. "Hi, there. Ready for lunch?" She waved two brown paper bags in the air. "Chad made us your favorite."

Her dad grinned, waving her in. "A juicy bacon cheeseburger with all the trimmings and jumbo size onion rings?"

She wiggled her nose. "Okay, second favorite. Two equally delicious but slightly less artery clogging chicken salad sandwiches and fruit cups." Her father wasn't going to have a heart attack on her watch.

"Did he throw in a cookie?"

She peeked in the bag. "Chocolate chip."

"I'll take it. Come on in."

Ashley set the bags on her father's desk and pulled out the contents, including paper plates, and napkins. Their having lunch together was a great idea. They could talk about the construction on the visitor's center, which Adam suggested would start as early as next week.

In addition to installing a new tea bar, she also wanted to create a WiFi lounging area this time around where guests could enjoy the tea and relax. Customers lingering a little longer could be good for business. Maybe they could even have Zoe supply them with baked goods to sell. She made a mental note to talk to her best friend.

"How's your eye?"

"Can't even feel the bruise."

She leaned in to get a better look. "What's going on with your face?"

"What do you mean?"

"Your cheek is all red. That wasn't there this weekend, was it?"

"It's nothing." He brushed off her concern. "Patty came by to help me around the house last week and did some shopping for me. I'm afraid I might have had a reaction to the soap she bought. Got it all over my legs, too. I threw the bar out, so it should calm down in a day or two."

"Well, your eye does look better."

"Doctor says it should be healed in no time."

"Good, we wouldn't want you posing with a black eye in any of Adam and Zoe's wedding pictures, would we?"

He chuckled in agreement. "No, we wouldn't. Hey, speaking of the wedding, I was wondering if you might like to bring a date?"

She blinked. "You want to set me up?" Well that was a first. Where had this come from?

"I was thinking you should bring Graham Carpenter."

A piece of her chicken salad lodged in her throat, and she coughed.

"Are you okay, dear?" Her father grabbed her water bottle and handed it to her.

"Thanks." She took a sip and coughed again. What was up with this sudden interest in her love life? "I don't think Graham and I are compatible."

"But I'm sure you've gotten to know each other over the last couple of months working on the expo."

"I'm definitely not his type," she said. "He prefers brunettes."

"I could call him." He thumbed through his Rolodex. "I have his business card somewhere."

Her dad was not going to ask Graham to escort her to the wedding. Besides, she was a grown woman for Pete's sake. She didn't need her dad finding her a date.

This conversation needed to end. She bit into her sandwich again, chasing it with a swig from her water bottle. "I'm kind of seeing someone."

"You are?"

She nodded.

"That's great." He chuckled and picked up his sandwich. "Who is the young man that I'll have to keep my eye on?"

"Jacob Sanders," she said, unable to mask the apprehension in her voice.

Sam put down his lunch and twisted in his chair. "When the hell did this happen?"

Wow. She wasn't prepared for such a strong reaction. Sure, she didn't think he'd be doing cartwheels, but his frozen stance with his back to her suggested he wasn't taking the news well.

"It started in San Diego." She stopped, not knowing what to say. Although she didn't need his permission to date Jacob, she wanted her dad to at least be excited for her.

It was probably a bad idea to bring it up. Especially since she and Jacob weren't exactly moving from bed buddies to full-fledged couple anytime soon if he kept blowing her off to fix tractors.

"Ashley, dear. You love me, right?"

"Of course, Dad. You know I do. Why do you ask?"

"And you know I would only suggest things because I have your best interest at heart. So let me call Graham."

Oh good Lord. She wasn't taking Graham and that was that. Why wouldn't he let it go? Should she tell him she'd witnessed the Seattle tea farmer with his hands all over another woman? That might shut her father up.

"Dad, you don't really even know Graham outside seeing him at industry events. Besides, did you hear what I said? I'm *seeing* Jacob." The conviction in her voice even surprised her, but saying the words finally out loud felt right, awesome even. She smiled as her body tingled with pleasure at her declaration.

"The deputy is not the man for you."

"But how can you say that, Dad? You don't even know him."

"Trust me, he's just like his old man, Joe. He's using you." Sam came around his desk and sat back down.

"Using me?" she repeated. His words struck a nerve. She couldn't say for a fact that he wasn't using her. She hoped not, but there were just so many questions she had that only Jacob could answer.

"Honey, think about it. Jacob's running for sheriff in a few years. How convenient would it be if his wife were a Whitman?"

"Whoa! Slow down. Who said anything about getting married?" She wrapped up her half-eaten chicken sandwich and stuffed it back in the bag. Her appetite was gone.

Her father handed her his cookie. "I'm sorry to lose my cool; it's just you mean the world to me, Ashley. I'd hate to see your heart get broken like ..."

"Like Mom broke your heart?"

"No, by someone who doesn't have your best interests in mind. You know, you'll always be my little girl."

Ashley attempted a smile. "I know, but Dad, it's my life. Regardless of how you and Uncle Richard feel about Joe, you can't forbid me to see Jacob."

He leaned back and folded his arms. "I can't?"

"No."

He shrugged. "You're right."

"I am?" She paused to regain composure. "Of course, I am."

"You caught me off guard. If you want to bring him to the wedding, go ahead. It's not like he'd be the first Sanders to ruin a party."

Ashley studied her father. Just like that, he had done a one-eighty? Unlikely.

He rustled some papers on his desk. "Look, honey. I know we've got business to discuss. Can we meet later today? I've got an urgent call to make."

"Sure, Dad. Rochelle's coming over to listen to a webinar with me on using social media to elevate your marketing platform."

"Good. Good. You two are going to work well together."

Grabbing the trash from their lunch, she paused in his doorway. "And about Jacob, who knows? Maybe once you get to know him, you'll both become best friends."

Two seconds later she turned to see her dad with his hands covering his face.

Or maybe not.

• • •

Jacob chatted with the cheery nurse who reminded him of his mother while he waited for Dr. McDonald. It had been busy in the hospital, and he'd already had to wait for more than an hour. He'd camp out all day for the information he suspected the doc could provide.

Despite Sam's insinuation yesterday, Alan was not their guy—Jacob was sure of it.

Though he never suspected his brother-in-law, he had called Colleen shortly after the attack to see what they'd been up to that night. He wanted to make sure both she and Alan had a solid alibi in case anyone started to point a finger at them as possible suspects. He'd been relieved to learn they'd spent the evening visiting with one of Colleen's old teachers, Pixie White.

Ashley's dad had been so eager to pin his attack on Alan. That had been Jacob's first clue that something was amiss.

His conversation with his dad about Sam's character helped to start outlining a motive.

Jacob reached for his phone, feeling an overwhelming need to hear Ashley's voice.

How he'd ended their conversation last night still weighed heavily on his mind, and he was ready to man up. To hell with the investigation. Whatever he learned today, he would keep under his hat.

He tapped her name at the top of his contact list and brought the phone to his ear.

"Hi, Jacob."

His heart pounded in response to her sweet voice. "Hey, how are you?"

"Great. I just had lunch with my dad."

"Sounds like fun. Listen, Ash. I know I was a bit preoccupied last night, but I was hoping we could hang out." He hit himself on the head. Not exactly how he wanted to ask her out for the first time. "Would you like to have dinner with me night?"

"I'd like that," she said. "But what about Colleen?"

"Colleen?"

"The tractor."

"Oh, right. Alan's got plenty of help on the farm. Turns out they don't need me." Truth be told, there was no way Colleen would ever let him around any of her equipment. Not after the time he'd accidentally loosened a belt on her truck that caused it to break down. She'd had to walk a mile that afternoon in a storm without her rain boots and then proceeded to call him every name in the book. "I'll pick you up around 6 p.m."

"Sounds good. I'm staying with Dad."

His eyebrows burrowed at that news. "Everything okay?"

"Yeah, I'm just helping him around the house. He's been a bit jittery since the assault. Patty and Uncle Richard have been stopping by, too."

Jacob tensed. He hoped to God he was wrong about Sam, and that Ashley's revelation about his sensitive skin was just an odd coincidence.

"Do you know where he lives?" Ashley asked, interrupting his thoughts.

"Um … yeah. Lake Emerald, right?"

"You got it. Last house on the waterfront."

"I'll see you then." He clicked off the phone, guilt washing over him. Could this situation be anymore fucked up? He was in love with the woman of a potential lead suspect for a series of crimes to bring down the most powerful family in town, and it just happened to be her family and her father. When did his life turn into an episode of *Dallas*?

"What brings you by, deputy?" Dr. McDonald greeted Jacob.

"Hi, doctor. I just have a couple questions regarding a case we're working on. Do you have a few minutes?"

"Sure." Dr. McDonald ushered him down the hall and into his spacious office. One wall held a book case filled from floor to ceiling with books while a plush brown couch was pushed against another. Man, did everyone in Emerald Springs have a nicer office than he?

"How are your parents doing?" Dr. McDonald took a seat.

"They're great. Dad's moving and shaking it up in Olympia."

"Good to hear it." He grinned. "I voted for him. So what can I do for you?"

"I understand you've been treating Sam Whitman. I was hoping you could answer a couple of injury protocol questions."

"Sam? No, I haven't seen him in months." The doctor looked up at the ceiling in thought. "I think it was last year around the holidays."

Jacob leaned forward, wishing he didn't have to ask the next question. "You haven't treated him for a bruised eye?"

"Bruised eye?" Dr. McDonald's eyes widened. "No, I haven't. Is he okay?"

"He's fine. It's healing rather remarkably," he said dryly. "He was jumped at Emerald Tea Farm by some hoodlum who broke into the visitor's center."

"Oh, my." Doctor McDonald buzzed in a nurse to bring him his patient's file. "I hadn't heard, but I just got back from vacationing in Utah with my family. It's quite possible that another doctor tended to him while I was away. Let's see what we can find out."

A few minutes later it was confirmed Sam hadn't been treated recently by any of the doctors in the hospital. Jacob wrapped up his conversation and thanked the doctor. The enormity of the information he'd learned weighed heavy on his shoulders as he exited the hospital.

Sam's black eye had probably come with instructions on how to wash it off.

Jacob had his insider. He'd give his left nut to let someone else close this case.

CHAPTER SEVENTEEN

Ashley checked her watch and finished getting ready in her dad's second-floor guestroom. Jacob would be arriving any minute. She smoothed her blue sundress, spritzed her wrist with some perfume that she now knew drove him wild, and headed downstairs.

She'd decided instead of going out, they should take advantage of the beautiful, cloudless night and eat outside at the lake house. She'd taken the afternoon off from work and made a simple pasta with mozzarella, along with fresh tomatoes from the farm. For dessert, she'd tried out a new Pavlova recipe courtesy of Rochelle, who swore it would be a huge hit.

Ashley skipped down the stairs into the kitchen and flung open the refrigerator, checking out the dessert. The meringue-based bowl of yumminess sat in front with its fresh whipped cream and sliced strawberries and kiwi. It made her mouth water.

There was also another surprise in the refrigerator. Chad had stopped by an hour ago to stock it with his new summer ale he and Jen were testing. Jacob would be pleased. So would her dad.

She stepped out onto the front deck and looked out onto the lake, waving at her father's longtime neighbors rowing by in their canoe. The pink sunset created a stunning contrast to the dark blue water. She loved summer nights in Emerald Springs.

And this night in particular.

This was the perfect place for she and Jacob to talk, and they'd have plenty of time alone since her dad had made an impromptu trip to Seattle this afternoon for business. He'd called her earlier to say he was too tired to drive back and decided to get a hotel for the night.

She couldn't wait for the deputy to get here. Maybe after dinner they could watch the sunset on the dock swing, then if that conversation went well, spend the rest of the evening at his house or her condo. She was determined that tonight they'd talk, but she wasn't totally crazy. Her body ached for his.

Just then, Jacob's cruiser pulled into the driveway. Her heart skipped a beat as she moved down the patio's wooden stairs and waited for him to get out of his car.

"Hi." She strolled over, stood on her toes, and wrapped her arms around him.

"Hi." He stroked her hair. She purposely wore it down, knowing how much he liked to lose his fingers in it. "You look beautiful."

She beamed at his compliment. He didn't look so bad himself in dark jeans and a white button-down shirt. Hopefully he wouldn't be too disappointed that she'd changed their plans without telling him.

"Do I smell like lilacs or pasta?"

"Definitely lilacs." He tilted his head. "Why would you smell like pasta?"

"Because I'm almost finished with dinner." She motioned for him to follow her inside. "Right this way."

Jacob followed her inside into the kitchen. "Is the pasta for Sam?"

"No, for us." She smiled up at him but noticed he didn't reciprocate. Was he upset? "Do you not like pasta?"

"Ash, no, it's not that." He shoved his hands in his pockets and glanced around the kitchen. "I had planned on taking you out to dinner."

"I know." She reached inside the cupboard for two dinner plates. "You didn't make reservations, did you?"

"No."

"Then it's okay. I just thought it would be nice to cook for you. Have dinner outside, even. It's such a gorgeous evening, and who knows how many more summer nights we'll have like this."

"Will your dad be joining us?"

"No." He had business in Seattle and decided to stay over. We've got the place to ourselves."

"He's doing better?"

"Yeah, appears so. I'm not sure why he's up there. Adam didn't mention it. It was a spur-of-the-moment trip to visit a business partner."

"Graham?"

Ashley scoffed. "I doubt it." She opened a drawer and grabbed some silverware. "They don't really know each other. Although, he wanted me to invite him to—"

"Invite him to where?"

"Oh, nothing." She motioned her hand, downplaying her father's suggestion. "It was silly."

Jacob leaned against the kitchen island, his face serious. "Tell me, Ash."

"He wanted me to ask Graham to Adam and Zoe's wedding." She reached over and grabbed some napkins. "Funny, right?"

"Hilarious," Jacob said flatly.

Moving toward Jacob, she gave him a playful swat. "I told him no, of course."

"Good." He stood silent for a few seconds. "I left something in the car. I'll be right back."

"I'll be right here," she quipped. What had he left in his car? Maybe he'd brought her flowers. She searched quickly for a vase just in case.

Jacob returned, no flowers in hand. "Everything okay?" she asked, slightly disappointed.

"Yeah. Just needed to check in with the sheriff. My phone was in the car."

"Well, dinner is nearly ready." She handed him the pasta bowl, and wedged a serving spoon inside. "Can you take this out?"

Jacob looked down. "You know, Ash. I was really hoping to take you out tonight."

"I know. I just thought it might be nice to spend some time alone. Minus my cousins or your sister …" She paused, adding, "… or my parents."

Jacob helped her bring dinner outside, and she finished setting the patio glass table. Everything looked perfect, if she said so herself. There was only one thing missing: Chad's beer for Jacob. "I'll be right back. I have a surprise for you."

She dashed into the house, grabbed a bottle of beer out of the fridge and bottle opener, and popped it open.

"Courtesy of Chad," she said, returning outside. She handed Jacob the bottle.

"Did he know I would be drinking it?"

There it was again. That hint of agitation in his voice.

"Well, we didn't talk about who would be drinking it." She sat back down and unfolded her napkin, placing it in her lap. "Jacob, is something the matter?"

"I think we should talk about us."

Finally. He wanted to talk. Although, by the way he blurted it out, she wasn't sure she'd like what he had to say. "I'm listening."

She braced herself for what was coming.

"I know what you're doing, Ash. We don't need to do this. I'm letting you off the hook."

"What I'm doing?" What on earth was he talking about? "Why do I need to be let off the hook, Jacob?"

He took a swig of his beer. "We should eat first. You went to a lot of trouble." He picked up his fork and took a bite of his pasta before setting his fork back down.

"Do you not like it? I could make something else." She stood and slipped on the flats she'd kicked off to the side. "Grill some burgers or we could order a pizza or something."

"No, it's not what you made; it's that you made it in the first place."

"What are you talking about?" She sat back down and crossed her arms. Jacob was making no sense, but clearly something she'd done had royally ticked him off.

"Ash, I asked you out on a date. To take you out," he said. "In public. This is not public."

"I'm sorry." She drew in a breath, not quite sure what she was apologizing about. "I just thought this place would be more private to finish our conversation from last night that we obviously need to do. Since you can't seem to do that, I guess this was a bad idea."

He shook his head. "I don't want to fight with you. We've done enough of that over the years to last a lifetime. I just want you to know that I get it."

"Get what? Jacob, I really don't understand what this is about." His beating around the bush was now starting to tick her off. He was worse than Zoe.

"You can't handle it that you're a Whitman and I'm a Sanders, and you don't want your family to know about us."

Whoa. Where had that come from? She threw her napkin to the side. "First of all, I invited you over here because I thought it would be fun to cook for you and give us privacy to talk. Second, I told my dad just this morning that we were—" She blinked back the tears threatening to reveal her true feelings any minute. "You know what. Forget it. You've obviously given this a lot of thought. I guess I know how little you think of me." Her voice quivered.

Jacob pushed his plate aside, running his hands down his face. "You may not even realize it, but I know you're having doubts."

She studied him. He wasn't completely wrong. She had worried what her family would think, but not because of his last name— because she'd hated this man most of her life.

When she shared the news with her dad earlier, it had stirred something inside her. Strong feelings for Jacob she sure as hell wasn't going to reveal now.

And he was one to talk. Why was he getting off the hook with the fact that he couldn't handle being in a serious relationship? "You know, Jacob," she said, coolly, "my dad warned me about you. Said you were using me. I'm starting to think he was right. This isn't about our last names, you're just looking for an excuse—any excuse—to bolt."

"Well, don't worry. I'm letting *you* off the hook." She threw his words back in his face.

He shoved his plate and started to stand but stopped. "You've got this all wrong."

"Do I, deputy? Jacob, you are incapable of anything beyond sex with a woman."

"That's not true."

"Sure it is, and instead of having the balls to admit it, you're putting the blame on me. The truth is I couldn't care less about your last name, but if that helps you walk away from whatever it is we were doing, then fine. Go ahead; believe that I'm a shallow, cold-hearted Whitman."

"Ashley ..."

"You got what you wanted. Apparently what you've always wanted. Why would you stick around?" Her eyes burned through his, demanding he answer the question.

Just then his pager went off and his face fell. "Shit. Of course this is happening now." He stood. "Ash, I've got to go."

"So go." She crossed her arms. "Don't let me stop you."

"I don't want to leave like this. I think we've both misunderstood some things."

She shrugged. "I understand things perfectly. I don't have anything else to say."

"Well, I do." He came over to her side of the table and bent down. His breath warmed her earlobe, causing her heart to race. "It was never just sex with you."

And with that he took off. Minutes later, she could hear his tires fly over the gravel.

Ashley grabbed her wine glass and moved to the wooden swing at the edge of the dock. She took a seat, pushed off, and stared out at the rosy pink sunset.

What had happened to the romantic night she'd planned? Clearly these misunderstandings—if that's what they really were—highlighted the one overarching problem: neither of them knew how to move this relationship forward. Not with its volatile foundation they'd each had a hand in sustaining with years of bickering and trading insults.

She downed her wine and looked out at the lake. Maybe her dad was right. Jacob wasn't the guy for her.

CHAPTER EIGHTEEN

Jacob took a deep breath, ready to get this procedure over. His eyewitness account of Graham and Carlos, coupled with Sam's faking his attack was enough information to issue a warrant to search Carlos's home and bring all three in for questioning.

Twenty-four hours after Jacob's visit to the hospital, the sheriff had sent him up to Graham's home and requested the Seattle police be on standby in case the tea CEO gave Jacob any trouble.

He hadn't meant to start a fight with Ashley last night. The surprise look on her face told him he'd been dead wrong about his assumptions. He felt like a complete ass. She'd gone out of her way to arrange a romantic dinner, and he'd accused her of having ulterior motives.

Nice job, idiot. He wouldn't blame her if she never spoke to him again.

This persistent feeling that he wasn't good enough for her was his hang up, and he needed to get over it.

He'd somehow tell her the truth when this whole mess was over—he'd never felt this way about any woman, and he'd been afraid she didn't feel the same way.

But right now he needed to concentrate on the task at hand and bring in this ass clown for questioning. When he'd gone out to use his phone last night, he'd called the sheriff. He didn't doubt that Sam's spontaneous trip to Seattle was to see his partner in crime.

It pissed him off that Sam was continuing to involve Ashley by encouraging Graham to be her date to Adam and Zoe's wedding. Could it be to provide an alibi? The whole Whitman clan would be together. Were they planning their next sabotage act on that day?

Not anymore. This game they were playing was over. Clenching his fist, Jacob knocked hard on the door. Within seconds, it swung open.

A confused Graham stood in a suit and tie on the other side. Jacob smirked. Did he wear that damn thing twenty-four seven? He'd be sporting a more industrial look soon enough.

"Jacob, what are you doing here? Is Ashley okay?"

Jacob tensed at the mention of her name. He really should be in Emerald Springs to protect Ashley when all hell broke loose even if she couldn't stand the sight of him. He intended to get back there as soon as he could.

"Graham, I need you to come with me down to Emerald Springs."

"What the hell for?"

"We have some questions about some recent activity at Emerald Tea Farm and—"

Graham slammed the door.

Jacob grimaced. Grabbing his phone, he called for backup. Apparently, they were going to do this the hard way.

• • •

Ashley tousled her hair in the bathroom mirror, adjusting her silky, pink feathers. Her Vegas showgirl costume that, in addition to the flock on her head, consisted of a tight, pink-glittered corset, black fishnet hose, and pink stilettos.

She patted the soft satin straps holding up her corset. It was time to get this show on the road.

After the fight with Jacob, the last thing she felt like doing was dressing up and celebrating with her family and friends. Far from it. She unzipped her purse and pulled out the note he'd left on her pillow in San Diego, eyes resting on the word "truth." *Jacob*

Sanders wouldn't recognize the truth if it bit him in the ass. She ripped up the note into tiny pieces and threw it in the trash.

Adjusting her feathers in the mirror one last time, she forced a smile. She just needed to get through this night and then she could crawl into bed and forget these last two weeks ever happened. Start fresh and avoid Jacob.

The problem was she didn't want to forget what they'd shared. All the romantic moments like the way he kissed her before he left San Diego or how he welcomed her home in the airport with her pompoms.

Ashley walked over to the dress rack Jen had wheeled into the Emerald Eats women's bathroom and flipped through its contents. It was filled with fun, sexy Vegas costumes for the female guests to wear if they'd like. In the men's bathroom was a similar rack with colorful polyester suits and fedoras.

Costumes had been Chad and Jen's fabulous idea.

She stepped out and walked down the short hallway to the main dining room. The neon lights Chad and Daniel had rigged up ricocheted off the walls, creating a true Vegas atmosphere.

In virtually no time, they'd pulled it off—a party that their bachelor and bachelorette were going to simply love.

She rolled up behind Chad, who'd donned a bright blue suit with matching fedora. "Nice work, cousin." They high-fived. "This place looks awesome."

In addition to the lights and party music, Chad had moved tables around, and she and Jen had created a special area for the ladies to enjoy their cocktails and makeovers. At the far corner, they'd rented a photo booth, which Ashley and Zoe's assistant, Courtney, had decorated to look like a tacky Vegas wedding chapel. Ashley also hired a fortune teller to walk around and read palms. Flipping over her hand, she sighed. Hopefully, the fortune teller could confirm that Jacob wasn't the man for her.

Uncle Richard and Patty were the first to arrive, followed by Caroline, the owner of the Coffee Queen, and Pixie White, the former elementary school teacher who had taught both Adam and Zoe.

Daniel came up next to her, letting out a low whistle. "Wow, Ashley. What poor guy are you out to slay?"

She pointed to her head. "I feel a little silly wearing these feathers."

"No one will be looking at your head." He laughed. "Good job tonight. You should come and work for me."

"Oh, I think you've got the best in the business," she said nodding toward Rochelle. Both Rochelle and Jen had decided to be cigarette girls from the forties. Instead of cigarettes, they were giving out raffle tickets and door prizes.

She eyed Daniel's standard black business suit. Rochelle had probably forced him to at least put on the black fedora he was sporting.

"See you dressed for the occasion."

"I had a late meeting about the resort expansion. No time to get my costume, and I'm not wearing any of those hideous numbers in the men's bathroom that Chad probably picked out."

"Your hat needs something." She plucked one of her feathers from her head and attached it. "Now you're ready, big boy."

He nodded. "Ready to take all of Adam's money if he ever gets here."

Ashley scanned the now crowded restaurant. Her gaze rested on Rochelle, who was chatting with Marlon. Whatever they were talking about, both were laughing up a storm. "That's an interesting pair."

"Yeah," Daniel agreed. "She really likes him. Adam asked her if she'd have coffee with the two of them and they hit it off. Her mom has addiction issues, too. Adam thought Rochelle might be able to help." He leaned in. "Marlon asked her to be his sponsor."

"Wow. That's great. He really is trying to clean up his act for Zoe, isn't he?"

Chad came up and fist bumped Daniel. "So, where's Jacob, Ash?"

"Why would I know?" Ashley asked.

"Oh, please. Like the entire town doesn't know that you two are sleeping together."

Ashley stood speechless. "Does that mean the whole family knows?" She glanced at a grinning Chad and then Daniel. "Well?"

"That my cousin is doing the nasty with my best friend? Yeah, the cat's out of the bag." Chad added, "As long as you don't do it in my kitchen, I think it's great."

Daniel nearly lost it and Ashley punched Chad's arm. "Well, you two don't have to worry. It's over."

"Really? You two would have been great together," Daniel said.

Ashley blinked. "You think so?"

"Absolutely. You're both smart, driven, a bit stubborn, and almost as attractive as me and Rochelle." He laughed.

Ashley couldn't help but smile. It was weird to hear someone else state what she and Jacob had in common, but Daniel was absolutely right. How could she have not seen that. "Maybe we could have been a good pair. It's just … Jacob thinks I have a hang-up about getting involved with a Sanders."

"Do you?" Chad asked.

"No, I couldn't care less about his last name, but say we got together." She paused, looking at Chad and then Daniel. "Does that make me a hypocrite?"

"Why would you think that?" Daniel asked.

"Well, I don't know. All of our lives we've hated each other."

"Sure it's hate you two were feeling?" Chad wrapped his arm around her, giving her shoulder a squeeze.

Her gaze trailed to the front door where her dad had walked in, waving his wallet. Someone was ready to play a round of poker or blackjack. "My dad will be happy it's over. He didn't take the news well."

"He'll get used to it," Daniel said. "That feud was years ago."

"Maybe, but Uncle Richard and Jacob's dad still aren't speaking to each other."

Chad pulled one of the feathers out of her hair, tickling her cheek. "Then maybe you and Jacob will finally give them a reason to start."

"That'd be nice ..." She wasn't so sure. She'd have to first convince Jacob that she didn't care about his pedigree and she wasn't as shallow as he had pegged her to be. Would he ever believe her?

Just then, Adam and Zoe entered the restaurant, hand in hand and all smiles. Their genuine excitement helped lift Ashley's spirits. She needed to stop brooding over Jacob, at least for the time being, and join in the fun. "You're here." She gave her best friend a big hug.

"Finally, big bro. Your two best men are going to take all of your money and leave you crying like a baby." Daniel head locked Adam, leading him to their poker area.

"Excuse us, ladies." Chad followed.

"Daniel, make sure Adam gets into his costume first," Ashley shouted and grabbed Zoe's hand. "Let's get you dressed."

Zoe giggled but looked a little horrified. "Will I be wearing an outfit similar to yours?"

"Better. I have a special one picked out for you." Ashley led her to the bathroom where the bride-to-be quickly changed out of her modest royal blue dress and stepped out of the stall.

Ashley squealed. "Oh, my God. You look so hot. Adam is going to absolutely die when he sees you."

Zoe eased up to the mirror to take a peek. The outfit Ashley chose for her was a beautiful white and gold beaded corset with a beige tulle train. Ashley had told her friend to bring her sexiest high heels, which of course, Zoe instantly complained about, being a flats kind of gal. Still, she managed to bring some nude heels that were perfect.

"I feel like I'm showing way too much skin." Zoe turned around to examine her back.

"That's because you are." Ashley grinned, reaching into her oversized purse. "There's just one thing missing."

"A trench coat to cover me up?"

"No, silly." She pulled out a beautiful, glistening tiara.

Zoe clasped her hands. "Oh, I've always wanted to wear one of those."

"And now you shall. I hereby crown you Princess Zoe." Ashley wedged the hairpiece into her best friend's head arranging the gorgeous, brown waves to fall to both sides. "Perfect!" Ashley giggled. "I hope Adam has enough dollar bills in his pockets to pay for his lap dance."

Zoe's eyes widened but then she shrugged. "He's got a few on him."

They headed back into the main room where a white-suited Adam scooped up his fiancée, obviously approving of her wardrobe change.

Thirty minutes into the party, Ashley grabbed her cocktail and escaped to the kitchen. Alone, she took a sip, enjoying the extra kick that also made her lips tingle. In addition to being a fabulous brewmistress, Jen knew how to mix her drinks.

Zoe popped her head in the swinging doors. "I was wondering where my maid of honor disappeared to."

"Just wanted to see about some more appetizers. Chad's staff are doing such a nice j—"

Loud shouting over the music ended their conversation, and both glanced at each other, concern washing over Zoe's face. "Oh, God. It's probably my dad."

They rushed out to see a male and female officer hovering around not Marlon but Ashley's dad. She sighed in relief. Leave it to Chad to hire male and female strippers. She should have known he would ignore her orders.

Daniel came up to Ashley and pulled her arm. "Let's go in the kitchen."

She yanked it away. "What and miss the show? Don't worry, Dad," she called out. "You're only arrested if they read you your rights, right, Chad?"

The female officer motioned for her to shut up and cuffed her dad.

"Sam Whitman, you have the right to remain silent … "

CHAPTER NINETEEN

Ashley shoved her hands in Jacob's leather jacket and yanked the feathers off of her head, throwing them to the ground. A lone feather stayed embedded in her long locks.

Jacob wasn't sure what his next move should be, but he definitely wasn't going to reach down and pull out the feather.

Tonight was going to be a long one, no doubt about it. All three suspects were now in separate interrogation rooms. The sight in front of him broke his heart.

"Ashley, why don't you let me drive you home?" Adam asked, bending down to pick up her feathers and toss them in a nearby garbage can. "You can change, and then if you really want to come back, I'll bring you."

She paced the length of the small break room. "I'm not going anywhere. I want to see him."

Jacob knew that was his cue to speak up, whether he wanted to or not. "You can't."

"Jacob, why is this happening?" Raising her hands, she gripped his uniform. "Did you know this was going to happen?" Her blue eyes desperately pleaded for an answer.

"Ashley …" The words died in his throat.

She let go of him, throwing her hands in the air. "Of course you did. That's why you left so abruptly last night."

"Jacob, what can we do?" Adam asked. "My dad is absolutely sick about all of this. The whole family is still at the restaurant waiting for answers. Is there anything we can tell them?"

Jacob took a deep breath. Grabbing Ashley's hand, he ushered her and Adam down the hall and into his office. Ashley plopped down in a chair, her pink corset peeking out from his jacket, which he'd given her to cover up with earlier.

It killed him that her world was about to change; he'd known about it for a few days, and there was nothing he could do to prevent her pain.

Would she ever forgive him for breaking the case when it would surely end in her dad serving time … possibly in a federal prison for the immigration hoax?

He shut his door, not wanting anyone in the station to hear their conversation. He might have a small office, but the walls were concrete. Now he could speak freely.

"I know your family is anxious to learn more. Sam's been taken into custody. They're asking him some questions. He'll most likely be here until bail is set."

"Doesn't he get a lawyer?" Ashley asked, wiping her eyes.

"He's already called one." Jacob handed her a tissue from his desk. He could get into a lot of hot water for what he was about to share, but he wanted her to hear the next bit of news from him and only him. He took a breath.

"Sam had an accomplice."

"Who?"

Jacob glanced at Adam, who nodded his approval.

"It was Graham."

Ashley flew off her chair. "What! This all has to be a mistake. Why, they barely even know each other. I know that for a fact. I'll give a statement."

Adam motioned for her to take a seat. "Actually, they know each other quite well."

"You knew, too?" She shook her head in disbelief.

"Only recently."

"So let me get this straight. My dad and the competitor I had a stupid crush on were in cahoots to take down Emerald Tea Farm? That doesn't make any sense."

"Ashley, I am just as shocked by the news as you," Adam said, resting a hand on her shoulder.

Jacob pulled up a chair beside her and took her hand. Adam's lame attempt at consoling her was starting to piss him off. "It's too early to know the motivation, but Graham incriminated your dad earlier tonight."

Adam clenched his fists. "Did Graham confess to everything?"

Jacob nodded. "All of it." Graham might be the mastermind behind the sabotage, but he'd cowered once he realized the jig was up. After the backup arrived, Jacob busted through the front door, and minutes later, they found a quivering Graham upstairs in the corner of his bedroom.

On the car ride to the Seattle police station, the CEO wouldn't shut up, placing all the blame on Sam. Since they'd arrested him for resisting to go with Jacob for questioning and read him his rights, everything he said could be used against him.

Adam began to pace, not taking it well that his uncle was behind all of the incidents. He stopped, his eyes burning with rage. "And Daniel? Did Uncle Sam order the hit on Daniel?"

Jacob looked over at Ashley. Her own eyes were void of any emotion.

"Answer the question, deputy."

"He didn't." He took a deep breath. "Graham fingered Carlos and said the custodian had gone rogue and had been following Daniel for weeks."

Adam sighed in anger. "So this Carlos was the guy who followed Daniel home after Chad's engagement party?"

"Appears so," Jacob said, "Neither Graham or Sam knew what Carlos was doing until after he jumped Daniel." He looked directly at Ashley. "I shouldn't be sharing any of this, but Graham confessed that Sam wanted out after Daniel's attack."

Ashley bolted from her chair, tears streaming down her face. "None of this makes sense. My dad would never do any of the things he's been accused of doing."

Jacob reached for her hand, but she immediately yanked it away. "Ashley, we have proof of Sam's involvement."

The moment he'd been dreading was finally here. *God, please help her understand that I am not the bad guy here.*

"What proof could you possibly have?"

"It was really a conversation we had that made me suspect he might be involved. I saw Sam's rash on his face—"

"What does that have to do with anything? He was allergic to the soap Patty bought for him."

He sighed. Another lie Sam had told to cover up. "It wasn't soap. It was makeup."

"Makeup?" Adam asked.

"I went to the hospital yesterday and talked to Dr. McDonald. Sam had never been treated for an eye injury."

"Jacob, what are you saying?" Ashley's voice quivered.

"He faked the attack."

• • •

Ashley stared out the window of Jacob's office. Adam had returned to the restaurant to update the family and suggest they all wait at Uncle Richard's until her dad's bail was set.

Was this just a horrible nightmare? Somewhere in this building her sweet, dear father sat alone in a tiny room, probably frightened out of his mind.

And Jacob was the one who put him there.

"Can I take you home?" Jacob asked. His eyes were full of worry, but that did little to console her at the moment.

No, she didn't want to go anywhere with him. "I don't want to go home."

"How about my place then? I could order some take-out."

"Jacob, my dad could go to prison. I'm sorry, but going home with you and sharing a pizza is not what I want to do right now." She stood and threw her hands up in the air. "If ever."

He leaned back in his chair and folded his arms. "Why are you mad at me?"

"How long have you known?"

"About your dad? Not long."

"So, basically, I tipped you off about his allergy to makeup and you suspected his black eye was a fake?"

"Yes, and there were a few other things."

"A few other things," she repeated. Great. There was more that he'd kept from her. She should have known. Getting mixed up with him had been a colossal mistake. "When did you suspect Graham?"

"Before we left for San Diego."

Her had flew to her mouth. "Oh, my God. Did you sleep with me to keep me away from him?"

"Ashley, that's ridiculous, and you know it. Was I prepared to keep him far away from you? Hell, yes. That's why I arranged our rooms next to each other." He reached for her hand. "What happened between us and how I feel about you has nothing, and I mean nothing, to do with any of this."

A single tear slid down her cheek. He reached out and tried to catch it, but she flinched.

She couldn't believe he didn't understand how frustrating this was for her. Her dad was in serious trouble. "Couldn't we have talked about your suspicion before you had him *arrested*?"

"Ashley, that's not how these things work. And even if I could, I was just trying to protect you ..."

Ah, so this was the price of being Jacob's object of protection. "Your protection came at the expense of keeping me in the dark, didn't it?" Her voice shook, but she was determined to get her next sentence out. "I don't want your protection if it means you keep secrets from me."

"Ashley, calm down."

"You want me to calm down? My dad is being interrogated and you did this to him!"

"First, he did this to himself. Second, your dad isn't above the law."

"But he's innocent. This has to be a misunderstanding, and if you had just talked to me, we could have gone to my father together and cleared all of this up. Instead, he's somewhere in this building shackled."

"He's not in handcuffs."

"That's not the point." This conversation was pointless, he'd never understand. No, Jacob may have thought he was protecting her, but if he really cared for her—or trusted her for that matter—he would have told her his suspicions.

"Ashley, come on. You're obviously in shock. If you won't let me take you home, at least let me walk you back to Emerald Eats." He reached out for her hand.

"No, don't touch me." She bit her lip. Didn't he hear what she'd just said? No, this was the real Jacob. He went around making up his own assumptions, not trusting her or what they shared. "You can't just thread your fingers through mine. We're not those little kids anymore. What I needed was the truth. You've never been good at telling me the truth."

"What are you saying?"

She squared her shoulders and raised her chin. "What I'm saying, Deputy Sanders is I will never make the mistake of getting involved with you again." She yanked off his jacket, threw it at him, and stormed out of his office.

• • •

Jacob wandered aimlessly through the Split Acres fields. When he started out on his walk, he thought he'd take advantage of the beautiful Sunday afternoon to clear his mind. His first day off since the arrests three weeks ago, it was nice to get away from the station and spend some time outdoors. This land had always been a place of refuge when he was a boy.

As he arrived at the area of Split Acres property that bordered Emerald Tea Farm, however, the pain that he'd been carrying around in his heart sharpened. He hadn't seen or spoken to Ashley since she stormed out of the sheriff's station. All of his calls went straight to her voicemail.

He knew from Chad, she was completely devastated over her dad's arrest and had been staying with Zoe. It killed him that he couldn't drive over to the bakery and comfort her.

If only he had handled things better. True, he couldn't talk about the case freely with her, but he sure as hell could have asked the sheriff to let him be the one to bring Sam in. He would have made sure it wasn't as public as what he heard went down in Emerald Eats.

Not that it mattered. Sam was guilty. Tomorrow he'd enter a plea bargain and learn his fate. Jacob wished he could be there for Ashley. As far as he knew, she hadn't been to the station to see her dad once the family decided not to post bail.

He didn't blame them. They were going to be further crushed when they learned the news that Graham had confessed to. Even though Sam wanted out, Graham had been blackmailing him to organize one final act of sabotage and destroy the Whitman tea crops while the family celebrated Adam and Zoe's wedding.

Jacob's anger bubbled up as he recalled Ashley telling him that her dad wanted her to bring Graham. Of course, it all made sense. Graham and Sam would have an alibi.

Now more than ever, he wanted to tell Ashley how much he loved her, how he'd always loved her. Had he ruined any chances to have a future with her? To get her back, he'd have to do something big.

His hiking boots kicked the fresh dirt as he looked around the land that he'd sold his shares of to Colleen. Bending down, he let the loose dirt run through his fingers while glancing over at the Whitman farm. This land was part of his heritage, but his heart had crossed over to the other side. How could he win the woman who possessed it?

He smiled hesitantly, knowing exactly what he wanted to do to get Ashley back—and it was huge.

CHAPTER TWENTY

Ashley flashed her first genuine smile in weeks as she watched her best friend walk down the aisle.

Zoe looked simply radiant in her long, flowing, white wedding gown. The strapless dress, with its sweetheart neckline, showed off her best friend's sleek frame.

She glanced over at Adam, who obviously couldn't take his eyes off of the most beautiful woman in the church. Chad reached behind Daniel and slapped him on the back. "She showed up."

Leave it to Chad to make a wisecrack. It was good to see all of her cousins smiling. The family hadn't laughed much the last three weeks.

Her father's arrest had sent them all into a tailspin. They learned that he and Graham had been working together to deliberately sabotage the Whitman business and brand, and that her father had been the one to organize the imposter immigration officials, a clear federal offense. Their plan all along had been to create havoc, slowly chipping away at consumer confidence.

Why her dad had turned his back on his family and concocted such a diabolical plan with Graham was still unclear. Ashley had attempted to visit him those first few days, believing he was innocent. He had refused to see her.

Graham and Carlos both confessed, leaving really no option for her dad but to take a plea bargain. All of them would be behind bars for quite some time.

With so much pain and heartache swirling around the Whitmans, Adam and Zoe were hesitant to go through with the wedding and even asked Ashley if she'd like them to postpone it.

She said no. How could she let her cousin and best friend delay their happily ever after? The family needed something good to celebrate.

As the couple now gazed lovingly into each others' eyes and recited the sweetest vows they'd written themselves, Ashley studied the guests who filled the beautiful church. Her gaze rested on a person she never expected to be there for her.

Her mother.

Shortly after her father's arrest, her mom had flown to Emerald Springs to be with Ashley, and she had no plans to leave anytime soon. At first Ashley resisted, but she finally realized she needed her mom now more than ever. They were far from winning any awards for mother and daughter of the year, but it was a start.

She smiled, watching her mom inch closer to a beaming Marlon. Her mom could flirt all she wanted, but it wasn't going to happen. Zoe's dad seemed to be sweet on Rochelle's mother, Rita, who'd arrived a couple weeks ago from Australia to help once the baby was born and was seated on the opposite side of him.

Chad, Daniel, and Adam. Everyone had gotten their happy ending.

Well, not everyone.

• • •

"I thought I'd find you here." Daniel took a seat next to Ashley. "Mind if I join you?"

Ashley shrugged and scooted over, trying not to wrinkle her dress. Not that it really mattered now. They'd just finished the wedding party pictures on the left bank of Emerald Paradise.

She'd decided to sneak away for a minute and gather her thoughts before the reception. The bench overlooking the sparkling blue lake had always been one of her favorite places on the property.

"I don't think I can smile for another picture."

"Me either." He laughed. "Let's face it, we're the two best looking Whitmans."

"Yeah." She couldn't help but chuckle. "Adam and Chad really didn't get our good looks, did they?"

"So how are you doing?" Daniel wrapped his arm around her.

"I don't know. Okay, I guess. I just needed a few minutes." She glanced at the stone plaque dedicating this area to her Aunt Sheila. "And to spend some time with your mom."

"I think she would want you to visit her today," Daniel said softly. Ashley knew he completely understood why she was here. He'd been very close to his mother, and Ashley suspected he also spent a lot of time himself in this very spot.

She sighed. "Aunt Sheila just knew how to say all the right things to make me feel better. Even when my parents fought, way before their divorce, she had this wonderful way of making me feel like I was part of your family."

"You are part of this family." He chuckled. "For better or worse."

"Yeah, why are my parents the worse?"

"Have you talked to Uncle Sam?"

She shook her head. "No. I don't know if I'll ever be ready."

"You know, no one blames you for what happened."

"I know." She'd felt so used and betrayed. Graham she couldn't care less about, but her father?

It sickened her.

"So, what about you and Jacob?"

"I don't think there's a me and Jacob."

"Still haven't talked to him."

"No. I know he was just doing his job, but I just can't understand …"

"Can't understand what?"

"That he couldn't tell me the truth from the beginning."

"Ash, there's some things he just couldn't share. Not with any of us."

"I know." She rested her head on Daniel's shoulder. "I want to believe you're right, but even if we could work through some of our communication issues, would his need to protect me always come with a price? If we got back together, would he feel the need to hide the truth from me again?"

She blew out a breath, not quite sure of that answer. "All he did was try to get the truth and then when he knew it, he tried to protect me." She sighed. "I returned the favor by ending things. I don't deserve him."

"I think you're missing the point in all of this," Daniel said.

She pulled her head up and sat up. "Which is?"

"You need to trust what's in here." He touched his heart.

She cracked a smile at her cousin, the hopeless romantic he'd become. "It doesn't matter. I haven't seen him in three weeks. He's probably moved on by now." Just saying the words caused her eyes to fill up. "I blew it."

Daniel turned his head toward the resort. "Hmm …you sure about that?"

Ashley shifted to see what Daniel saw.

"I think I'll be going now." He stood and adjusted his cuff link. "You know, the mud room's available if you two don't feel like going to the reception."

"Bye, Daniel." Ashley's heart pounded as she watched Jacob walking toward her. Halfway there, he shook hands with Daniel.

And he looked incredible dressed in black slacks and a sports coat.

"Hey." Jacob said, shoving his hands in his pockets.

"Hi."

"You look beautiful."

"Thank you."

"How was the ceremony?"

She glanced down at her pink, strappy sandals; a little mud from the morning's rain had caked on her heel. They could do this chitchat or she could ask him the question of the hour. "What are you doing here, Jacob?"

He sat down, stretching his legs. "I've been asking that myself since I pulled in."

Her back stiffened at his uncertainty. "Maybe you should listen to your instincts," she said coolly.

"You're absolutely right. I think I will." He grabbed her hand and pulled her up. Before she knew what was happening, he lifted her high off the ground.

"Jacob put me down."

"Not this time. We're going for a little field trip."

"But we're at a wedding, and I'm the maid of honor. I have responsibilities." She tried to break free, but he was holding on too tightly.

"Zoe will understand. They'll think we're off having trashy wedding sex. Isn't that what all maids of honor are supposed to do?"

They would not be having sex, but nevertheless, she stopped struggling and took the moment to enjoy the cologne she'd missed inhaling these last three weeks.

She couldn't deny his hold made her body tingle, but where were they going?

•••

"Jacob Sanders, why did your drive me out to this open field when I should be at my cousin's wedding with the rest of my family doing the flippin' Electric Slide?"

He laughed at that image and kicked at the mud on his front tire. "I'll take you back soon enough. Be careful of that hole over there." It was a wide hole that had taken him a day to dig once he'd gotten Colleen's permission. With some help from Alan and all three of the Whitman brothers, it was exactly as deep as it needed to be for the time being. He reached in the back of his squad car and pulled out her pompoms. "Remember these?"

"You can't just show up with pompoms and expect me to jump into your arms." She paused and crossed her arms. "Not again."

"I knew you'd say that," he said, grinning. He'd played this moment out in his head several times over the last week. Her reaction was exactly how he envisioned it.

"No you didn't."

"Well, I suspected it. Stand right here." Moving to the back of his trunk, he popped it open and pulled out two of his sister's shovels.

"What are those for?"

"You'll see." He propped them up against his car, careful not to scrape it.

She folded her arms, eyes narrowed and ready to shoot darts any second. "I want to go back to Emerald Paradise right now."

"In a few minutes. Now here's what I need you to do." He handed her her pompoms and then went back to the trunk where he retrieved a basketball, but not any basketball. This one he'd used to make that record three-point shot ten years ago. Today he'd be giving it up, but for a greater purpose.

"What? Are we going to pretend we're in high school?"

"Not quite." He came up alongside her, both of them standing at the edge of the hole. "Okay, when I say three, throw your pompoms right in there."

She arched her eyebrow and leaned down to inspect the hole. "Seriously?"

"Yeah, like this." He demonstrated the posture. "Like you're about to make an award-winning shot."

If I do this, will you take me back?"

"Yes."

She sighed and bent her knees.

"Perfect."

"Have you lost your mind?"

He brought the basketball up to his face, palms flat on the nylon. "Just like this."

"Fine." She threw her pompoms in, not bothering to mimic his posture. "Well?"

He took his basketball and threw it in the air. It landed right next to the pompoms. Exactly where he'd hoped. On top of them might have been bad karma. Instead, they were side by side in this little venture. "Now we shovel."

"What are you trying to do? Bury our history? I'm so out of here." She stormed to the car, but he'd locked it.

"We're not done yet." He picked up one of the shovels and brought it over to her. "Here."

"Jacob, I'm in a bridesmaid dress, in case you didn't notice. I'm not shoveling dirt with you."

He smiled. "I did notice and you've never looked more beautiful. Now shovel."

"No."

Her eyes started to water and she immediately turned her back to him. Oh, God. He'd made her cry. "Ash, I'm sorry, I just thought—"

"Maybe you want to bury our history and forget it, but I don't."

"That's not what I'm doing."

"Then what is this?"

"You've got this all wrong." He picked up a shovel and handed it to her. "I want to build our future."

"By throwing our history in a dirt hole?"

He smiled. "I think I need to explain. This land is mine. Colleen sold it to me for my shares. When she gave it to me, I hadn't the foggiest idea what I wanted to do with it, but I do now."

"Which is?"

"I want to build my life with the woman I love. We just need to lay our foundation."

"My pompoms and your basketball?" She blinked.

"It's where it all started, right? I can't think of two better things that symbolize us. I love you, Ashley Whitman, and I know I screwed up by the way I handled things with your dad, and even before that with my own hang-ups about my family." He paused. "I'm sorry. Please say I haven't lost you."

The wind whipped through her hair as he watched her gaze down at the hole and then over at the Whitman Farm in the distance. He'd picked this spot because although it was on Split Acres property, it overlooked the place he knew she held close to her heart.

He took a deep breath and handed her the shovel, knowing what she did next with it would determine their future.

•••

Ashley threw the shovel to the side and kicked off her heels. Two could play this game. She crouched down next to the hole and took a deep breath. It was time to take Daniel's advice and trust her heart.

She jumped in and the mud squished between her toes. She reached down and scooped some in her hand. "Jacob, are you just going to stand there?" she called up.

Suddenly he appeared at the ledge. "Um … having fun?"

"As a matter of fact, I am." She reached behind her head with her mud-free hand and pulled out the clips holding her hair up, letting her waves fall loosely over her shoulders. Much better.

"Need some help?" He reached down and offered his hand.

"Yes." She grabbed his wrist and yanked hard, catching him off guard. He lost his balance and tumbled into the hole on top of her. The moist dirt tickled her back.

"Now we're equals." She swiped his face with her finger, leaving a muddy trail. "No more thinking you're beneath me, Jacob

Sanders. I'm not that childhood princess who thinks she's better than everyone else or that high school cheerleader who needs to be saved from a cheating boyfriend. Got it?"

"Got it." He stroked her messy hair. "Who told you about the boyfriend?"

"Chad set me straight. The point is, I don't need rescuing."

"I'll always protect your heart."

"I know," she said softly.

"But I'll never keep the truth from you again."

"I believe you." She ran her hands up and down his arms, knowing he wasn't talking about some stupid high school boy this time. "I shouldn't have blown up at you at the station like I did. I know you had a job to do."

"I understood. I never meant to hurt you," he said, stroking her hair.

I've missed you, Jacob."

"I've missed you too, baby." Jacob brought his lips down to hers, but there was something else she needed to say.

"If we're going to be totally honest, I've been keeping something big from you."

"Oh, really?" He sat up and pulled her onto his lap. Even though her dress was ruined, she appreciated the chivalrous act. He reached over and swiped a tiny smidge of dirt off of her face. "I think I know."

"You do?"

"You have a fetish for mud."

"No." She threw back her head and laughed. "Well, apparently I do, but it's not that."

"What is it, Ash?"

She grew silent and threaded her fingers through his. Bringing their joined hands to her lips, she planted a soft kiss on his knuckles. "I love you, Jacob Sanders."

And there it was. The words lodged in her heart had finally been released.

"I love you, too, beautiful." He wrapped his arms around her and held tightly.

"I don't know if you can call me that since I'm covered in dirt."

"You've never been prettier." He cupped her face and moved his mouth over hers for a long, sweet kiss. When their lips finally parted, Jacob was the first to speak.

"Ashley Whitman, will you marry me?"

Her hand flew to her heart. She'd never expected the question in her wildest dreams, but there it was. "Oh my God. I'm getting engaged." She flung her arms around his neck. "Wait until I tell Zoe!"

He rubbed his hands up and down her back. "Um … first you need to answer my question, Ms. Whitman."

She loosened her grip and planted several short kisses all over his face. "Of course, I will marry you, Deputy Sanders."

They kissed in celebration a few minutes more, then she turned around on Jacob's lap while he rested his chin on the crook of her neck. "I'm sorry I don't have a ring or didn't wait until we were back at the resort."

She laced her dirty fingers through his, an act she knew would symbolize their love for many years to come. "But you dug me a hole." She squeezed his hand. "And mud is kind of our thing. Although I think Daniel imports his. Next time, we might want to use the mudroom."

He chuckled. "I'm going to hold you to that. Speaking of which, I need to get you back to the resort."

She grinned. "Maybe we should clean up first."

"Excellent idea." He hoisted her to her feet, and then cupped his hands to offer her a boost. "Shall we, my fiancée?"

Jacob's fiancée. The most wonderful feeling washed over her. This was really happening.

Her cousins, his sister, and her best friend had all found their happily ever afters. It was now her and Jacob's turn.

When they finally climbed out of the hole, Ashley couldn't resist taking one last look at the basketball and pompoms they'd left behind.

This was their foundation. A new and stronger WhitSand partnership had just formed. She knew they both would move heaven and earth to make sure this one lasted forever.

EPILOGUE

One Year Later

"Okay, ladies! Shake what your mothers gave you." Ashley walked around the spacious aerobic studio at Emerald Paradise and slapped Jen on her butt. "We've got a wedding to get ready for."

Zoe giggled from her folding chair on the sidelines.

"And you … Mrs. 'I'm seven months pregnant so I'm just going to sit here and look cute' Whitman." She reached for Zoe's hand, pulling her up. "There's no reason why you can't be doing some of these exercises, too." After she demonstrated a couple of simple ones in the mirror that Zoe could easily replicate, her best friend groaned but then began to mimic the moves.

"Geez, Ashley, who knew that out of all of us you'd be the bridezilla?" Zoe huffed.

"I did!" Rochelle raised her hand.

"Just for that, everyone who isn't pregnant will be doing pushups next. You can all thank the Aussie for the pain you're about to be in."

Thirty minutes later, Ashley excused her maid of honor and bridesmaids to hit the eucalyptus steam room and enjoy one spa treatment on her. She had been a bit of a drill sergeant, but it was her wedding, after all, and it was only a week away. She wanted everyone fit and tanned for the occasion, even if she had to spray it on them.

After a quick shower and change of clothes into something more conservative, she headed into the lobby, passing the spa boutique. Pride swept through her as she stopped in front of the window. Her new "Touch of Ash" cosmetic line promptly displayed. Emerald Paradise was one of many luxury resorts carrying her new line, and Daniel had his staff give complimentary makeovers with the makeup. Her products were selling like hotcakes in spas up and down the West Coast. She had finally made her mark.

Spotting Daniel in the lobby looking as handsome as ever in his latest Armani suit, she greeted him.

"Looking good in the aerobic studio, Ash. Why don't you come work for me full time as my fitness instructor?"

She smirked at his offer. He'd never give up trying to steal her away from Adam. "Hmmm … I'll have to think about it." She added, "You know what's really looking good are your renovations. Rochelle gave me a tour of the gong vibration healing room earlier this week. Such a fabulous way to honor Aunt Sheila."

"It is pretty awesome," he agreed. "It's like Mom brought Rochelle into my life so I could bring this new technique to Emerald Paradise."

"I bet she did." She winked and pointed to the sky. "And I wouldn't be surprised if Aunt Sheila had a hand from up there with your happily ever after, too."

He grinned. "So, you'll never guess who's staying here next week." Leaning down, he whispered the Hollywood A-lister's name in her ear.

"No way! I'm so going to camp outside his room."

"Better not let the deputy hear you talk like that."

"We're not married yet." She glanced down at her watch. "I should probably go. Give that sweet baby boy of yours a kiss for me."

Daniel beamed. "Will do. Rick loves his aunt Ashley." He paused. "Oh, speaking of people who love you. Dad and Patty are having breakfast on the patio."

"I'll pop out and say a quick hello." She gave Daniel a peck on the cheek, and he disappeared into his office.

"Hi, everyone." Ashley walked over to the table. Uncle Richard and Patty were laughing it up with Marlon and Rita, who evidently had joined them for breakfast.

"Ashley!" Uncle Richard stood and hugged her. He pointed to her gym bag. "I see you're teaching your Zumba class. Do you think I have moves?" He wiggled his butt, arms flapping every which way.

"We'll work on it, Uncle Richard." She laughed. "I'm looking forward to seeing all of you tonight at family dinner."

"We wouldn't miss it for the world," Patty said and everyone around the table agreed.

Uncle Richard pulled her aside. "You know, this is going to be the first time Joe and I have shared a meal in twenty years."

"Why do you think we're only serving finger foods? No knives," she kidded. "What's this?" She picked up one of the colorful brochures with a cruise ship on the front from the table.

Uncle Richard sat back down. "The four of us our going on a South Pacific cruise this December. Now that I'm officially retired, it's time to get this party started." He winked at Patty.

"Oh, really?" Ashley asked.

Patty grinned. "You know it'll be summer there then. Isn't that right, Rita?"

"Yes, it's lovely back home that time of year," Rita confirmed.

"Well, it sounds divine." Ashley checked the time on her watch again and her heart grew heavy. She would be late for her monthly appointment if she didn't hustle. "I'll see you all tonight."

A round of nods, a quick goodbye, and she was off.

Ashley headed to her car ready for the familiar two-hour drive. Six months ago, with the help of Jacob and the support of her mother and family, she'd taken the trip for the first time to visit her father.

That reunion still weighed heavily on her heart. They didn't talk at all during that hour but held hands and cried the entire visit. After that, she came back the first Wednesday of each month to see him.

Over time, he admitted that he had got caught up in what Graham had ultimately promised: an opportunity to lead a tea farm, something he'd never gotten from her uncle.

Through his therapy sessions, he was finding it easier to express how he'd felt like a failure most of his life in his career, in his marriage, in comparison to his brother, and as a father.

Uncle Richard and her dad were rebuilding their relationship, too. What they discussed when they were together stayed between them, but her uncle had admitted to her he should have helped nurture his brother's career.

It didn't happen overnight, but he'd forgiven her father and promised things would be different from here on out.

Her dad now took responsibility for all of his actions. He vowed when he was released years from now, he would spend his remaining days making everything up to his family. He hadn't meant things to escalate like they did and never had wanted Daniel or any member of his family harmed. Still, he accepted he bore some of the blame for getting involved with Graham and Carlos in the first place.

Ashley believed him with all her heart. She knew it was a long road, and even if he was released early, there were many years of counseling ahead. She'd be there for him.

Arriving at the familiar prison, she was led to the visiting room where she stared at the white cement walls in silence. Minutes later, an officer brought in her dad. Although she'd seen him a half dozen times, it never got easier seeing him in his regulation prison clothes.

"Hi, Dad."

"Ashley!" They were allowed to hug when he arrived and before they took him away. She held him tightly.

"How are things?"

"Good." He chuckled. "I'm learning how to cook this week."

"Oh, really."

"Do you remember the time I tried to make filet mignon for your birthday at Richard and Sheila's place?"

She laughed, recalling that he'd almost set Aunt Sheila's kitchen on fire.

They spent the next twenty minutes catching up on the month. He'd been excited to share with her that he was selected to lead a new program to teach some of the other prisoners how to read.

They also talked about the wedding. It took her a few months to reach the decision to tell him about it, but she wanted him to share in her and Jacob's happiness even if he could only do it in these short visits. It tore her apart that he wouldn't be there to walk her down the aisle.

Their hour soon came to an end and an officer popped in to take her father away.

"Well, kiddo. I'm proud of you." His eyes filled with tears, and Ashley rushed into his arms.

"I love you, Dad."

"I love you, too, Ashley. Promise me you'll bring video and pictures next month? I want to see my new son-in-law in a tux."

She couldn't wait to see him in it, too. "I promise."

She watched as he was led out of the room. There was a real difference in her dad. In a weird way, with each passing month, he seemed happier than she'd seen him in years. His confidence was growing, but it wasn't the cockiness he showed before. She could tell he was making a contribution while in prison, and that made her happy.

She'd make good on her promise and bring an album full of wedding pictures next month, although she might have to pull out the ones of her mom.

Her mother. Elizabeth had moved to Emerald Springs permanently and was now managing the Coffee Queen. A bit ironic since it represented the final straw in her parents' marriage when her dad had purchased the then fledgling coffee shop. Now that place was all her mother could talk about.

Ashley left the prison and headed for the highway toward home. Though it was way in the future, one day her dad would be in the passenger seat making the trip back with her. She'd then help him rebuild his life. That father/daughter allegiance would never change and had only grown stronger over the last six months.

• • •

Jacob marveled at all Colleen and Alan had accomplished in one year. Their greenhouses were up and running, and the floral trade business was going quite well. He'd enjoyed the tour Alan had given him this afternoon. "You two have done an amazing job. Thanks for the break on our wedding flowers," he teased, bouncing his smiling niece on his lap. "Kaylee, your parents are rock stars."

Colleen plopped down on the sofa next to them, kicking off her lavender rain boots decorated in an odd plant pattern.

Jacob eyed the boots. "Are those marijuana leaves?"

She rolled her eyes. "They're tea leaves, you idiot. Geez, I thought you'd recognize a tea leaf by now. I had them made for Ashley, but they were so cute, I got a pair for myself. Tell any of those Whitman boys you saw me in them, and I'll kill you."

"Mum's the word." He reluctantly handed over his niece. "I need to head out. See you tonight?"

"Wouldn't miss this family dinner for the world. Someone's got to make sure Daddy is on his best behavior."

"Who would have thought Ashley and I would be bringing our dad and Richard together after all these years?"

"Let's just hope what happens tonight doesn't start another twenty years of fighting."

"Amen to that." He kissed Colleen and then Kaylee. "See you soon."

Leaving the house, Jacob hopped in his squad car and backed out of Split Acres. The rain from earlier had stopped, and the sky had opened up. How symbolic. It had to be an omen that tonight would go well.

So many good things had happened this year. Ashley's cosmetics line had taken off, and he couldn't be more proud. His talented fiancée had also helped Jacob realize his own dreams of running for sheriff. In two years, he would be setting those plans in motion. He'd put his all into the race, and if he won, it wouldn't be because he was married to a Whitman but because he was the right man for the job.

A man who loved this town and the residents of Emerald Springs, and would always care about their safety.

He shifted gears, grinning at the black hair tie around his console. In just over a week, its owner would be his wife. They just had to get through tonight.

Jacob pulled in to his driveway and took the next hour to shower and to change into khakis and a dark blazer. In no time, he found himself parked outside Ashley's condo. They alternated staying in his house and her condo until their new home was finished, which would be sometime this fall before the snow fell.

She stepped out in a strappy black dress that he remembered far too well. He had removed that dress from her soft shoulders right around this time last year. With a closet full of little black dresses, he suspected she'd purposely chosen that one for tonight.

"Nice legs." He whistled and was greeted with a slow, sexy kiss.

"It's your lucky night." She flashed a smile. "They'll be around you later."

He ran his fingers through her hair, enjoying the scent of her shampoo. He suspected it was tea-infused. He was learning there were compromises in any marriage and he'd have to get use to a life with tea—a lot of it.

"We could skip tonight."

"And miss seeing your sister eat at a Whitman establishment for the first time? Fat chance!"

Jacob drove them the short trip to Emerald Brewing Company, the new name for the former Emerald Eats. The microbrewery had opened last fall and was an instant sensation.

Newlyweds Chad and Jen were proving to be real movers and shakers in the organic craft brew world, making a name for themselves and their microbrewery. They'd gotten married last November, opting for a small outdoors ceremony on the Whitman farm during the fall foliage.

Jacob held the door for Ashley as the crowd inside cheered and clapped at their arrival. Zoe waddled over and whisked his fiancée away while Adam, Daniel, and Chad playfully kidded with him about what they'd do if he ever hurt their cousin. He had no intentions of that ever happening.

He laughed and joked with the eco-engineer, the Armani model, and the nature nut. He couldn't wait to spend family gatherings with these guys, just like they did all those years ago before the feud.

Ashley and Zoe returned a few minutes later with beers for Adam and him, while Chad and Daniel headed toward the kitchen.

Ashley pointed to Zoe's stomach. "I really hope you make it to next Saturday. Are you sure you're only seven months pregnant?"

Adam and Zoe looked at each other, matching grins.

Jacob took a swig of his beer. "You two have the classic 'we're hiding something' look. I see it all the time in my line of work."

Ashley squealed. "You're not, are you?"

"Should we say it out loud?" Adam asked, smiling down at Zoe.

Zoe rubbed her hands up and down her belly. "We're having twins!"

"Oh my God!" Ashley threw her arms around Zoe. "Boys or girls?"

"One of each."

"Good job, Adam." Jacob slugged him.

"We're going to tell Dad and the rest of the family after your wedding," Adam said. "We didn't want to commandeer your celebration."

Ashley continued to share in the awesome news with Adam and Zoe while he searched the crowd for his parents. He thought they'd be here by now.

Without warning, Ashley's mom came flying over, flinging her arms around his middle. Thankfully Colleen and Alan were also making their way toward him. Saved by the bell. He gave Elizabeth a quick kiss on the cheek and greeted his sister.

It was nice to see Colleen taking a break from the farm and all gussied up. He whipped out his phone and snapped a *selfie* next to Colleen.

"What are you doing?" Colleen asked.

"Posting this on Facebook for the world to see."

She narrowed her eyes and leaned in. "Do and I'll tell everyone that you slept with a Barney night-light until you were thirteen."

"Deleting right now." With one swipe, the photo was gone. He'd take another when she wasn't looking.

He glanced around the packed restaurant. Everyone they'd invited had arrived except for two. "Do you think dad and mom decided not to come?"

"They're here."

"They are?" He glanced behind his shoulder. No sign of their father or mother. "Where?"

She nodded. He couldn't believe he'd missed it. There in a corner booth sat his parents with Richard and Patty.

Colleen shrugged. "Chad said they came early to talk with Richard, and they've been in that booth for the last three hours."

"Really?"

Just then, Ashley came up next to him.

"Looks like our families are getting along," he said, not really sure if that statement was true. "Should we go talk to them?" He felt Ashley's fingers thread through his and they stood together, hand in hand, just like they'd done as kids, once again bracing for the lion's den.

"I've got an idea. Let's start with a toast." Ashley motioned to Chad, and a minute later the catering staff appeared with trays filled with champagne flutes. Daniel clinked his glass to silence the crowd.

"Thank you all for coming to our family dinner," Ashley started, taking a flute. "We Whitmans have been having family dinners since … well since I can remember, but tonight Jacob and I wanted to celebrate this tradition with both of our families and our closest friends."

Richard moved forward with his glass. "Ashley, dear. May I say a few words?"

Jacob gulped and looked at his dad, who now stood next to Richard. He'd been too young to remember firsthand, but the last time they'd all toasted with champagne it hadn't gone well.

But on this occasion, clearly something had changed. Both his father and mother had flutes in their hands and huge smiles on their faces.

"Jacob, I've known you since you were in diapers," Richard began.

Jacob smirked, feeling a little awkward that now everyone in the room was envisioning him in Huggies. "I've watched you play with Ashley, irritate her, infuriate her …"

They all chuckled and Ashley piped in, "But in a good way, honey." She wrapped her arms around him.

Richard continued, "And you've always looked out for her. My niece may have only figured it out last year, but Joe, Rebecca, Sheila, and I always knew it would be you two who would fuse our two families together."

Jacob smiled at Ashley, who had tears in her eyes. He pulled her in close and wrapped his arms around her. "We're destined to be together," he whispered in her ear.

Richard patted his dad on the back. "Joe, we did good in our prediction."

"Yes, we did," his father agreed. "It might have been the only thing we agreed on."

Jacob laughed because he knew his dad would get a snarky comment in. However, the way he and Richard were carrying on, the feud just might be over.

Richard raised his flute and all of their loved ones around them followed suit: his parents, Colleen and Alan, Adam and Zoe, Daniel and Rochelle, Chad and Jen, Marlon and Rita; Patty, Elizabeth, and all of their dear friends, sharing this special moment.

"To Ashley and Jacob. May this WhitSand partnership last forever."

His father clinked his glass to Richard's. "If it's anything like the original one, it's going to be one hell of a ride." He paused, a twinkle in his eye. "And the best one of your life."

A Sneak Peek from E
merald Springs Legacy, Book One
Adam's Ambition by Monica Tillery

Adam Whitman twirled his favorite Mont Blanc Starwalker in his fingers, enjoying the weight, and smiled to himself. This deal and the promotion that went along with it were as good as his. The partnership between Eco Initiatives and Everlight Optics would be the biggest contract he or anyone else at the company had ever brokered, and if he could just get the woman across from his desk to sign on the dotted line, it would be done.

"You're telling me you were a farmer? As in, you were out there in the field, picking tea leaves?" Christine Grazioli, Everlight Optic's CEO, shot him a suggestive smile from her spot on the sofa in his office.

He'd seen that look before, and if he played his cards right, the ink would be dry on the contract by noon. "I certainly did, from the time I could walk until the day I left home. My family owns the largest tea farm in Washington. You've probably had some yourself. Hold out your hand." He paused and picked up a crystal bowl on the table, holding it out to her. "Pick one."

She plucked a leaf from the bowl and handed it to him. He gave her a conspiratorial smile and turned the leaf over in his hand. "Nice choice. It says that an important decision you make will bring you much success." He dropped the leaf above her hand, letting it float gently into her open palm.

Christine laughed, throaty and seductive. "I don't think that's how tea leaf reading works. You're supposed to brew these and read what's left behind after I drink the tea." She glanced at her watch. "Oh, shoot. I've lost track of time. I need to get across town for a meeting at Paramount. Can we get in touch later?"

"Absolutely. I'll have the contract sent to your office; just send it back when you've reviewed everything and signed." He stood and opened the door. Once his client was safely down the hall, Adam fist-pumped the air in silent celebration. All it took was a nice working lunch and some harmless flirting, and he was on his way to closing a six-figure deal and locking in the promotion. This partnership would make the Eco Initiatives higher-ups very happy and guarantee him one fat end-of-year bonus. He laughed to himself; sometimes it was too easy. The tea leaves always did the trick. Women either believed in the magic or allowed themselves to think there was something between them. Who would have thought his upbringing on the family tea farm would still come in handy? He returned to his desk to review the paperwork so he'd be ready when she sealed the deal.

"Mr. Whitman, Richard Whitman is on line one." His assistant's disembodied voice came through the phone speaker, and he looked up from the proposal. How long had it been since he spoke with his father? Weeks at least. Far too long.

"Thank you, Lauren." Adam pressed a button on his phone and answered the call. "Hi, Dad." He sat back in his chair and relaxed, ready for a long chat. The deal with Everlight Optics would still be there when he finished with his family. He hadn't given them enough time lately. Or for the last several years, if he were to be honest with himself.

"Hey, son. Is now a good time?" The voice came through the line robust and hearty. It was good to hear him sounding so upbeat. They exchanged pleasantries until his father reached the real reason for his call. "I need you to come home."

Adam sat up straight. "What's wrong?" Fear gripped him and his blood ran icy in his veins. His father had asked him to come home once before, and only once. That time his mother's illness was taking a turn for the worse, and he had barely made it in time to say his goodbyes before she passed away.

His dad laughed. "Relax. Nothing's wrong. I'm looking to retire, and I could really use your help. Do you think you could get away for a week or two?"

A week or two? He would be lucky to make it through the weekend without getting a call about something. His job at Eco Initiatives left little time for any semblance of a normal life. When he wasn't busy with his own accounts, he was consulting on others or researching the latest technological advances in environmental sciences. His days were spent helping local L.A. businesses green their operations through technological improvements, training company sustainability officers, and consulting for lobby groups. He enjoyed working for Eco Initiatives so much, he rarely took vacation days and regularly worked sixty-hour weeks. Still, losing his mother taught him that he'd regret squandering his time when his family needed him. Once someone was gone, they were gone forever. If his father was asking him to come home, Adam knew better than to second-guess it. He never wanted to look back and wish he'd chosen differently.

"I could come up for a few days, probably. I don't know about a week." If his hunch was correct, his father wanted him to consider taking over the farm. His father had made no secret of the fact he wanted his eldest son to claim his place at the head of the family business, Emerald Tea Farm, to live out his legacy. He had heard it all his life and had resisted the pressure. His dad was getting older, and with no replacement in line, it might be more difficult to work it out this time. There was no chance that could be managed in a week.

"Adam, I need you, and I don't think we can wrap it up in a few days. I want to settle everything while I'm still able. I don't want to end up with a situation where I'm forced to hand everything over to the first willing body because I'm too old to do anything about it. Now will you come help me or not?" His voice was strong, determined.

"What about Chad and Daniel? What do they have to say about all this?" His younger brothers still lived in Emerald Springs and ran the family's other businesses. They would never come out and say it, but he always suspected they resented the assumption he would take over the farm, the family's lifeblood, when he was the one who left. Chad and Daniel remained loyal to the family in ways he simply hadn't, and they likely wondered why their father wanted Adam to come home so badly.

"Chad is busy with the restaurant, and Daniel has his hands full with the resort. They both say they're willing to help with the farm, but honestly I don't think either one of them has the time for it. They'd let the whole thing run into the ground before they'd admit they're not up for the job."

He laughed. His father was right; they would drop from exhaustion before they would ask him for help. "That's true, but what makes you think it'll do any good for me to be there?"

"Maybe you can talk some sense into them and help them realize they need to leave it to someone else, or maybe you'll come up with some way they can juggle everything. We might end up hiring someone to oversee operations, someone who doesn't have other businesses to worry about. That can only happen after we let the boys decide they can't do it, though. They'll never accept someone else if they don't get their fair shake first. Who knows? You might finally decide to join the family business."

His father rarely brought up the possibility of hiring an outsider to take over, and Adam took notice. If they were addressing the matter directly, Dad might finally be ready to retire for real—and had given up on Adam taking his place. He was surprised to feel the first twinges of disappointment and quickly dismissed them. He didn't want the farm. He had spent his entire childhood dreaming of leaving town and never picking tea again. He should welcome his father finally moving on, so why did it feel like something was being taken from him?

"I haven't worked in the fields in years, Dad. I don't know how much good I could do," Adam stalled.

"You know how little actual farming I do nowadays, right?" He could hear the smile in his father's voice. "I'm not exactly out picking tea."

"Yeah, I guess I can't remember the last time you really got your hands dirty." He sat back in his chair and stretched. "All right, Dad. I haven't taken vacation time in a while, and I suppose I can always work online if anything urgent comes up. I'll be there. I can probably swing five or six days." He clicked his mouse and scanned the calendar on his computer to be sure nothing pressing would keep him from visiting Emerald Springs.

"Thank you. This means a lot to me." Relief colored his father's tone.

"It's no big deal. Just give me a couple of days to get ready, and I'll be there. I'll let you know when I have a flight to Washington."

They ended the call, and he tapped his pen on his desk blotter, mentally calculating how much time he'd need before he could leave town with a relatively clear work schedule. The sooner he went to Emerald Springs and got everything squared away, the better. The nagging thought that his life wasn't tied up as neatly as he thought ate away at his confidence.

Over the past fifteen years, he'd held out hope his brothers would manage to work together to keep the farm in the family, but the other Whitman enterprises must be commanding too much of their attention. Daniel had always preferred the family resort, a perfect match for his attention to detail and appreciation for luxury, although Chad's work at the family restaurant was surprising, given that he excelled at the art of dodging responsibility. Adam had known tea farming since he could walk, and now he was in the position to take the company to another level. The farm had always been all-organic, but Richard couldn't fracture his focus enough to commit fully to both optimal farming and green operations. Adam could come in with fifteen years of education and experience and a fresh perspective, ready to revolutionize things.

He didn't actually want to leave his life and job in L.A., but now that he had time to dissect their conversation, Adam wondered why his father hadn't tried again to convince him to come aboard? It was probably best this way, best that his family held no unrealistic hopes or expectations of him. This way he could go home for a brief stay, do his part then get back to his life. So why did it feel like he was trying to convince himself? Could it be a small part of him longed for the life he always felt destined to live? No, surely not. He had worked tirelessly to create his new life; there was no way he longed for a return to the farm.

A senior partner stepped in from the hallway and rapped his knuckles on the doorjamb, interrupting his thoughts.

"Hey, Adam, you got a minute?" he asked.

He shut the browser window on his computer and stood, straightening his tie. "Sure, Mr. Campbell. Come on in. Can I get you a coffee or water?"

"Call me Mark, and no thank you, I'm fine. Please, sit." The partner came in and took a seat opposite him.

Adam sat but didn't relax as he waited for Mark to speak. He tried for an expression that said he was loose but confident. "I wanted to talk with you about your future at Eco Initiatives today. We've been watching you for a while, and you have an excellent record here. You're innovative, personable, and efficient. We appreciate your commitment to the environment and to the clients, and we feel that nobody else would be better suited for the position of accounts management for all of California."

He leaned back, ran his fingers through his hair, and blew out a long breath. "Wow. This is quite a surprise."

Mark laughed. "It shouldn't be. You've worked hard, and we think you're ready for the next level. Of course it comes with a lot more responsibility, but the compensation package will reflect that."

"I am flattered, really. This is an amazing opportunity. Would you give me a little while to think it over?" With this promotion, his dream job really, so close within his grasp, Emerald Springs seemed miles away. Strange how things could change so drastically. Just moments ago, he had almost allowed himself to consider taking over the farm.

Mark put his foot back on the floor and looked Adam in the eye. "Sure, of course. Take your time. I'll send over the details so you can see what you'd be getting yourself into, and you let me know what you think."

Adam stood as Mark did, and they shook hands. "Thank you, sir. I appreciate your faith in me."

"You earned it." Mark left, and Adam paced the length of his office, jingling change in his pocket, shocked by the news.

The Emerald Springs Legacy Series

Follow the Whitman and Sanders families in their continuing saga as they confront old rivalries and discover new love while protecting their legacy at the Emerald Tea Farm. Look for these upcoming installments in this exciting new continuity series from Crimson Romance:

Adam's Ambition by Monica Tillery

Colleen's Choice by Holley Trent

Chad's Chance by Elley Arden

Daniel's Decision by Nicole Flockton

Ashley's Allegiance by Robyn Neeley

To learn more about the Emerald Springs series, visit our website for more details, author interviews, and a special free prequel story.
http://www.crimsonromance.com/featured/
announcing-the-emerald-springs-legacy-continuity/